"Now stand up," he urged, reaching up to hold her hand as she did. "And shout, 'I am strong.'"

She hesitated for a moment, not because she didn't want to do as he instructed, but because this was a perfect place, a perfect moment, and she didn't want that to change.

"Do it, Layla," he urged. "'I am strong.'"

Smiling, she nodded. Then drew in her breath and shouted, "I am strong." And her voice echoed back to her. *Strong…strong…strong…strong.* For an instant the monkey chatter stopped, and the birds went silent, and all she could hear were her words. "I am strong," she whispered. Then shouted again, "I am strong." *Strong…strong…strong.* And closed her eyes to take in only her voice. *Her voice.* Nobody else's.

"You always have been," Arlo said. "You just never knew that."

She smiled down at him but didn't speak as there were no words to say to the man who'd just given her the world.

Dear Reader,

I live in a city with one of the most acclaimed medical schools in the world. Within a mile of my house, in any direction, there are more medical facilities than anybody could imagine, with about four hundred different offices and one hundred hospital beds.

Mike, my friend, practiced medicine out of the back of his Jeep, going from town to town, in some very isolated areas just a few hundred miles from my house. He lived a tough life doing it, the way my hero Arlo has done. Because of Mike, I wrote this book about a very compassionate doctor who never worked in a proper office or experienced anything convenient in his practice. That kind of medicine is still out there, even though it's not so visible, and my characters Arlo and Layla are lucky enough to find true love in the middle of the very difficult and isolated medical situations they've chosen for their lives, not unlike Mike, my inspiration for this story, did.

As always, wishing you health and happiness.

DD

Dianne-Drake.com
Facebook.com/DianneDrakeAuthor

NEW YORK DOC, THAILAND PROPOSAL

DIANNE DRAKE

HARLEQUIN® MEDICAL ROMANCE™

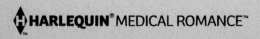

ISBN-13: 978-1-335-64181-6

New York Doc, Thailand Proposal

First North American Publication 2019

This edition published by arrangement with Harlequin Books S.A.

For questions and comments about the quality of this book, please contact us at CustomerService@Harlequin.com.

HARLEQUIN®
www.Harlequin.com

Printed in U.S.A.

Books by Dianne Drake

Harlequin Medical Romance

Sinclair Hospital Surgeons

Reunited with Her Army Doc
Healing Her Boss's Heart

Deep South Docs

A Home for the Hot-Shot Doc
A Doctor's Confession

A Child to Heal Their Hearts
Tortured by Her Touch
Doctor, Mommy... Wife?
The Nurse and the Single Dad
Saved by Doctor Dreamy
Bachelor Doc, Unexpected Dad
Second Chance with Her Army Doc
Her Secret Miracle

Visit the Author Profile page
at Harlequin.com for more titles.

To Mike Cramer, one of the hardest-working and best doctors I ever knew. The world is a little less bright without you, my friend. RIP.

Praise for
Dianne Drake

"This is a classic romance…a lovely story which I heartily recommend."

—*Harlequin Junkie* on
The Nurse and the Single Dad

CHAPTER ONE

"I KNOW WHAT we were, Mother. But two years deserves a better ending than what we had, and when this opportunity came..."

Dr. Oliver Benedict, Layla Morrison's boss, mentor and, yes, Arlo's grandfather, had three spots open for volunteers—specifically the three candidates he was looking at to be his new assistant chief of surgery.

"No, I don't know if Arlo knows I'm the one Ollie picked for this assignment. It's only been five days from the time he gave me the nod until now, and Ollie specifically said communication with Arlo wasn't always available. So, yes, I might be a surprise."

But the need was legitimate. According to Ollie, Arlo was alone right now. His medical assistant had gone home to India for a while and after living with Arlo for two years herself, and listening to him talk about the way he wanted to practice medicine here, in Thailand, Layla knew what she was getting herself into.

Jungle medicine. Nothing easy. Nothing convenient. It was hard work. Sometimes backbreaking. And it was so embedded in Arlo's heart it had caused their break-up. Two years into their relationship and the call of the jungle had beaten her.

"No, I don't know if this will give me a lock on a promotion, but it will finally give me some closure. We didn't have that. It was too difficult at the end and we were both hurt. So, I'm hoping that this will help me, maybe even Arlo, finally move on."

Layla had had one disastrous attempt at a relationship after Arlo and had compared everything Brad did against the way Arlo had done it. Nothing *could* compare, though, and now it was time to fix that so she could finally move on with her personal life since the professional side was rolling along quite nicely.

Layla was one of the top general surgeons in Ollie's practice, highly regarded for her skills, in line for a promotion. That part was just what she wanted and, finally, she had time to look beyond that, to having a life outside medicine. Except there was Arlo. She hadn't been able to shake him off. Not in the physical sense, but in the emotional. All the what-ifs? They wouldn't let go, so now it was time to purge them and move on.

Layla sighed loudly enough for her mother to hear. "Look, it's only two months, then I'll be home and hopefully in a new position. Ollie hinted that I'm the forerunner. So, please, just wish me luck here because working in a jungle hospital scares me a little bit." But not as much as facing Arlo after all this time.

"Yes, Mother, I'll be careful. And tell Daddy thanks for the SUV. The way these roads are turning out to be, it's exactly what I needed." Her dad had made a couple of phone calls and, just like magic, it had been waiting for her at the airport. But he had connections here in Thailand. In fact, he had connections everywhere so what he'd done for Layla had been easy. Everything her parents had ever done for her had made her life easier. Which was one of the reasons Arlo had always called her spoiled. She'd taken advantage of that from time to time. Until Arlo had pointed that out.

Still, her parents always supported her in what she wanted to do. Sometimes the support was a little grudging, since their ideas of what they wanted for her were entirely different from what Layla wanted for herself. But there hadn't been a time since she was a little girl that she'd seen herself as anything other than a doctor, and now Layla was on her way to do some doctoring in the jungle with a man who'd been her partner for two years. Talk about an improbable situation.

"Two years," she said out loud, as she swerved to miss a rut in the dirt road. Arlo Benedict had been at her level during their medical residency, and the arrangement to share an apartment had been a practical one. For Arlo, it had been about money. His grandfather, Ollie, had been supporting him through school, but just barely, since his own surgery was quite costly to operate. And Arlo's parents—they were like Arlo was now. Jungle doctors, living on practically nothing.

When Layla had first met Arlo, he'd been struggling. Not complaining, though. But his life had been hard, and he hadn't had many extras. No going out with friends for pizza and beer. Working an extra job when he'd really needed to be studying. He had been so dedicated—dedicated in a way she'd never seen in anyone, and she admired that. Plus, he was easy on the eye, and maybe she'd had a little crush.

She didn't know for sure, but when she'd mentioned she had a bedroom to rent, he'd jumped at the chance. Layla had told herself that having someone there was simply a matter of practicality. But in the case of asking Arlo to be her roomie, it had possibly been something more. Certainly, she'd been open to suggestions at the time. He had been smart, drop-dead gorgeous and quite emphatic that he'd be gone once his residence was completed.

Arlo had come with everything she'd wanted, and something she hadn't wanted—a long-term relationship. She hadn't been about to tie herself up that way until she'd started climbing the ladder, and that had still been a long way off.

Well, she had been wrong about the relationship. Just being with Arlo had made her want to be with him all the more. No, he had not been a long-termer and, yes, he had been clear he wouldn't stay. But being with Arlo for two years had changed her. Made her want things she hadn't known she wanted. Made her want Arlo in ways she'd known he hadn't been available.

Had it been the challenge of him, or the allure? Probably some of both. But when her real feelings had started getting in the way, the allure had taken over in a big way. Not that it mattered because, in the end, he'd left her. It was always his plan, he'd told her. But she'd truly thought she could change his mind.

Unfortunately, Layla couldn't. And their ending had been bad. Arguments they'd never had before. Shouting. Crying. Naturally, she'd blamed Arlo for everything but, deep down, she'd always known she couldn't hang onto him. She'd just tried ignoring it.

Initially, Arlo's resistance at accepting her offer, and he did resist, had been quelled by her declaration that theirs would be a friends-only situation. Sure, she'd wanted more. Which, as it had turned out, had been the case with Arlo as well. And within two weeks a cozy night when two weary surgical residents had shared a bottle of wine and a bowl of popcorn on the couch had turned into…

Of course, there'd been early morning promises that what they'd done was a one-time thing. Except it wasn't. For two years. Now, nearly five years down the road, while Layla was perfectly on track with her career, Arlo was the loose end she needed to tie up because she didn't want to be alone for the rest of her life. Because she was a total washout when it came to relationships—just ask Brad, her only attempt at another relationship after Arlo. Then there was the whole ticking of the biological clock thing going on. Yet she couldn't take that step forward because—well, she was blaming it on their lack of closure, even though they'd both known, at the start, that Arlo would eventually go one way and she another.

It had seemed easy enough when they'd

talked about it, but when the time had come, it wasn't. Had Layla loved Arlo then? Yes, in a lot of different ways. But had she loved him enough to give up her dreams to follow his? No. Absolutely not. And neither had he been prepared to give up his dreams for her.

So, why was she here? To be honest with herself, she'd jumped at the chance before she'd thought it through. And once she'd committed, she wasn't going to back down. Her plan—her only plan—to earn this promotion was do everything required to move her forward.

To back out of two months in a Thailand jungle hospital with her former lover would shove her back, not push her forward. So, here she was, feeling a lot of trepidation about Arlo's reaction if Ollie hadn't contacted him yet, and scared to death of a two-month commitment that, at one point in her life, might have turned into a lifetime commitment, had things worked out differently.

As her dad always said, *Whatever it takes to get you to the next level.* And while Layla didn't know if this assignment would do that, it would certainly allow her to experience a side of medicine she knew little about. That, if nothing else, was a good thing as it would help make her a better doctor. So in two months she could be a better doctor who'd finally shut the door on an old relationship. It was good. All good because she needed Ollie to see she was a team player. Sometimes she wasn't. Layla knew her reputation—she could be a little aloof, sometimes standing alone.

But growing up the way she had, with a photojournalist father who made documentaries all over the world, and her mother a film actress who, like her father, worked all over the world, she'd learned to be independent at a young age. Sometimes she could be too independent, which wasn't necessarily in her best interest all the time. Even she recognized that. Although Arlo had pointed that out as well. More times than she cared to remember.

Still, most memories Layla had of her parents were of one or both of them walking away from her, going off in pursuit of their careers, which, if nothing else, had been the impetus for her independence. Arlo walking away had simply shored up what was already there—the notion that she wasn't worth hanging around for. And for Layla, hiding behind the stone wall of independence she'd built around herself was easier than risking another rejection. She'd assumed that over time she'd learn to be happy there. Well, happy enough.

But sometimes the memories of a bottle of wine and a bowl of popcorn and what that had started did slip in. They hung on more tenaciously than almost any other memory of her life. And it was because of that memory Layla had been stalled in a place where there was no room for her. Where she wasn't wanted. A place she had to fix and move beyond.

While this trip to Thailand to work with Arlo had been providential, it was also necessary. It was her chance to prove to herself that the feelings she'd had for Arlo were simply feelings meant only for that time and place, and had no bearing on anything else in her life. Then, and even now.

So, where was she anyway? Normally a quick check of an online map site was all Layla needed, but there was no cell reception out here, let alone a road that had been charted on a map. So she was only guessing she was headed in the right direction. A direction where she didn't expect modern facilities, let alone the basics like running water and electricity.

That's what Arlo had told her he'd come from, and that's what he'd always said would be the kind of place he would practice his medicine. He'd grown up in the jungle, traveled with his parents, who were both doctors. And it's what he'd said he wanted for his own life as he simply fit there better. Shortly, she would see if he did.

Layla looked ahead of her, saw a man rid-ing atop an elephant and nearly ran herself off the road staring at him. It wasn't the elephant that got her, though, not even the crater she swerved to avoid hitting. It was the wavering turn out of the swerve that wobbled her back and forth across the road. Unfortunately, it resulted in her landing in a drainage ditch with a flat tire, the front end down, back end up. Royally stuck and—she checked her phone even though it was pointless, and the result was what she expected—there was no way to contact anyone, anywhere.

"Damn it," Layla huffed, throwing her phone back into the car as she stood alone on the road, trying to figure out what to do. "No bars. Not a single, lousy blip on the bar indicator." Her first test out here, and she was already failing it.

After walking around her car several times, assessing and reassessing the situation, Layla finally sat down in the dirt, hoping someone would come by to help her. Someone in a truck with a tow rope, she hoped. Maybe even Arlo? But the only person who did pass was a withered little old man with a pushcart filled with fruits and herbs. He smiled graciously at her, then began a long-winded discussion, none of which she understood. After he finished speaking, he tipped his straw hat to her, picked up the hand grips of his cart and meandered on down the road at a pace that would favor a snail in a race.

"Well, so much for that," Layla said, deciding to hike on down the road and hope that somewhere along the way she stumbled on someone who could help her. Or maybe even stumble on the village itself.

An hour later, making very little progress due to the road conditions, Layla stopped to rest, sitting down on a roadside rock and watching some kind of wild pig munching the droppings of a papaya tree. And this was why she and Arlo hadn't succeeded at their relationship. They'd talked about it *ad nauseam* for the last few months they'd been together. While she'd never been in the jungle, she could see it in detail through Arlo's description. There were good people here, leading extremely hard lives, in a place where nothing came easily. Transportation was limited, according to Arlo. As were communications. It was his passion, and she didn't condemn him for it. But it wasn't her passion. She wasn't the kind of person who could survive here. Even two months were beginning to seem like an eternity.

"You and your passion, Arlo," Layla grumbled, as she stood to resume her hike. Much to her surprise, the little man with the pushcart was coming back into view. Slowly.

Was he coming to rescue her? Her knight in shining armor? A man with a receding hairline, bushy gray eyebrows and some wispy chin fringe?

Naturally, when he arrived at her side, he was already chattering words she still didn't understand. His gestures were clear, though. She was to climb into the part-empty cart and be pushed wherever he wanted to take her. "Village by the big fig tree," she said, knowing he wouldn't understand the English interpretation of the village's name. But she couldn't pronounce it in Thai and any mispronounced attempt might land her someplace she didn't want to go, so she pointed to a small fig tree sapling off the side of the road, then attempted to gesture a much larger tree. Wouldn't Arlo just laugh at her now, standing in the middle of nowhere playing a game of charades?

"Big fig tree," Layla said a couple of times, even though the man had no idea what she was saying. He smiled, though, let her charade herself into more embarrassment before he gestured her to the cart again. Her taxi was waiting, and she couldn't have been happier to see it, despite the prickly straw in the bottom, and the caged chickens she had to share her ride with.

Oh, and the dog. The little old man had picked up a scraggly, lap-sized brown and white mutt somewhere along the way.

So, forcing a gracious smile, Layla climbed in, found a spot among the other passengers and shut her eyes. All those years ago, when Arlo had walked away from her, calling her too damned ambitious, it had hurt, even though it was true. Today—right this moment—she was glad her ambitions had kept her in modern society, as this was simply too hard already, and she hadn't even started.

Maybe it was what Arlo wanted from his life, living here and practicing jungle medicine, and maybe he was one of the most benevolent, altruistic and humane people she'd ever known, but none of this was for her, and if she hadn't known it then, she surely did now.

"Of all the doctors in the world, he sent you?" Arlo shook his head, not in disbelief so much as amusement. "You working in the jungle is as improbable as me working in a modern hospital somewhere. But you've certainly got the skill I need, so..." He visibly bit back a laugh. "Welcome."

Layla opened her eyes, which she'd purposely kept shut so she could avoid the full picture of her impetuous volunteering, and there he was, taking away her breath the way he always had. Only maybe a little more since the jungle setting made him seem…better.

Tall, roguishly handsome as ever and a little weathered, which became him. His blond hair looked sun bleached, and it was long, still with its gentle curl. She'd always liked those curls and the way they had felt in her fingers. And the penetrating blue eyes that still penetrated. But the thing that had always attracted her most were his dimples. Honest-to-gosh sexy dimples when he smiled.

"I'd have made my grand entrance differently if I could have, but I suppose this works," she said as she picked straw from her hair. "Oh, and to answer your question, yes, he sent me."

"He didn't tell me it was you he was sending," Arlo said.

"Probably because he was as surprised as I was that it was my hand that went up first to volunteer. Also, because he couldn't get in touch with you."

"Ah, yes. It's all about the soon-to-be-open assistant chief position, isn't it? When he told me he was going to announce it, I assumed you'd be the one fighting to get to the front of the line. Didn't count on Ollie sending you out here as part of your climb up his ladder, though. Especially since we haven't spoken in five years."

"Three," she corrected. "We spoke that time you came to New York to visit him."

"One word, Layla. You said hello in passing."

"And you acknowledged it by bobbing your head and grunting."

"That's not exactly speaking."

"I was civil," she said, trying to right herself in the cart, wishing Arlo would help her out so she wouldn't look quite so undignified. But he was standing back, arms folded across his chest, the way he'd always done when they'd argued. So, was he expecting this to turn into an argument? "And in a hurry."

"You were always in a hurry, Layla. And I'm assuming it's paying off, taking on more and more just to prove yourself to him."

"Not denying it," she said.

"Nope, you never did. I think I saw that in you the first time we met."

Of course, Arlo could see what he wanted to see in her. That was part of their fundamental problem. What he wanted versus what she wanted. Or, in their case, needed. "Part of my basic make-up, I suppose. But I never heard you object," she said, stepping out of the cart, trying not to disturb the chickens while also trying to shoo the dog back in.

"Probably because I didn't object. I liked your ambition. I was raised by pacifist parents who took things as they came, which is pretty much my style. Someone with your kind of ambition—I don't recall ever seeing it in anyone before you. Not living in the jungle for as long as I did. It was an eye-opener for me, and also… well, sexy."

Layla turned to thank the old man for the ride by bowing to him, then tucked a few Thai coins into his hand which he pocketed eagerly as he returned her bow, then scurried away with his cart. "Right up until the day you walked out." She brushed the straw off her backside, then stood at the bottom of the rough-hewn wooden stairs and looked up at Arlo. "It's two months. You need the help, I'm available, and—"

"And in the bargain it makes you look good because you want that promotion. You haven't changed, Layla. I'll give you credit for that. Where you are now is where you were when we split. Still trying to climb that ladder."

"I'm not the only one in the running."

"No, but you're the only one who'd come to Thailand to impress him. That's huge, even if you don't want to admit it."

"I also came to see a side of medicine I've never seen." And try to make things right between them—things that seemed like they were already off to a shaky start.

"I offered you that. Remember?"

"For a lifetime, Arlo. You wanted a lifetime commitment and we weren't even..." Layla wanted to say *in love*, but that was implied. Their relationship had been about many things, but love had never been mentioned. In fact, because of their circumstances, she was sure that was the reason it never had been mentioned. It was too complicated. It got in the way. There were no compromises that would work for both of them. Even though her feelings for him might have been—well, that didn't matter now, did it?

"Anyway, Ollie's deal is for two months. I couldn't have done a lifetime, Arlo. You knew that from the beginning. But I can do two months, and you do need that help. So this is good for both of us. You get an extra doctor for a while and I gain extra knowledge." And closure, because she really did need to move on, and the only way she could think to do it was ending things better with Arlo.

But for Arlo? She'd spent too much time wondering if he'd needed more at the end the way she had. Now she had two months to find out, and put things into proper perspective. Then, hopefully, close the book on that story once and for all.

"Do you really think that helping the boss's grandson will get you any special notice? Ollie's not like that, Layla. In fact, it could go against you, volunteering to come here, when he knows how badly we ended. He could look at it as being very manipulative. I mean, if I were in his place, I might."

"Or he could look at it as a way for me to improve my skills." And, keeping her fingers crossed, she was on the inside track because of her work. Nothing else. "So, in the meantime, I've got my medical bag with me, but my personal bags are in my car, which is stuck in a ditch somewhere between here and God only knows where. Do you know someone who can go get my car unstuck and bring it here?" She looked up at the sign over the door behind Arlo and smiled. "Seriously, you named this place Happy Hospital?"

They'd actually named this hospital together years ago. They were being silly one night, and maybe a little drunk, and the pillow talk had turned to the kind of hospital where each of them could see themselves in the future. Naturally, Layla had described something large and state-of-the art, whereas he'd simply said he wanted to work at a happy hospital. She hadn't remembered that until now. Apparently, he hadn't forgotten it. In a way, it made her feel flattered that he'd thought of her.

"Things are simple here, Layla. I know you're not used to that, but that's how we are. And the hospital name fits because when we don't have enough insulin to treat all our patients and don't have the means to go get it for another week or two, or when some other hospital like this one is ahead of us on the list, pushing us down the waiting list, we can either go all gloom and doom over our situation or try to make the best of it. Being happy with what we have helps."

"I didn't mean to imply it was a bad name, Arlo. But out here, in the middle of the jungle, it just seems—out of place."

"People are just as happy here as they are where you come from. It's all relative to their expectations."

"But are you happy here, Arlo? I know you always said this is what you wanted, but sometimes I've wondered what might have happened to you if you'd gone into your grandfather's surgery the way he'd wanted, or accepted any of the offers you had."

"I was happy here when I was a kid, traipsing around from village to village with my parents, and I still am. It was the choice I had to make because I wouldn't have been happy anyplace else, practicing any other kind of medicine."

He'd never doubted his decision either. He'd lived the traditional life for a while, and he'd lived this life. Ultimately, this was where he wanted to be. Where his heart was. And when he and Layla were together, that had always been the thing she couldn't, or had refused to understand. Accepting a position elsewhere might have been easier, but easier didn't mean better. At least, not for him.

"Anyway, I don't really have good sleeping accommodations for you. Tallaja, my assistant, usually sleeps in the ward when we have patients or the office when we don't. He's pretty flexible about that, but I'm guessing you won't be."

"As long as I have mosquito netting, it doesn't matter."

"Seriously? You've been doing your homework, haven't you?"

"I don't step into things blindly, Arlo. Except maybe our relationship."

"I never considered it being blind. Not one day of it." Arlo stepped aside as Layla marched up steps and pushed past him into Happy Hospital, brushing up against him just slightly, but enough to raise goosebumps on his arms. It was a familiar feeling—one he didn't want to have.

But every time she'd ever touched him, even innocently like just now, she'd caused that reaction that would, inevitably, lead to another reaction, then another, until… Damn. Why these thoughts? Why now when he was just coming to terms with the fact that he would never have enough to offer anyone else a decent life?

Even when he had been with Layla, Arlo had always known she would come to her senses about who he was and what he'd never have to offer her. It hadn't stopped him from getting involved, but it had always held him back from getting too involved. Back at the beginning, he'd drawn his own line in the sand then taken good care never, ever to step over it, except for that one moment near the end when he'd asked her to come to Thailand with him.

Stupid mistake. He'd known that as the words had come out, and he'd still felt the sting of her rejection a week later when he'd walked away, even though he'd always known how she would answer if he'd asked. "So, look around. There's not much to see, but it could be a lot worse."

Layla stopped just inside the hospital door, looked around and turned back to face him. "How many people can you accommodate?" she asked.

"Ten on the worst day ever. We do a lot of our treatment in-home because people here prefer it that way. But for the most part we dispense our medicine and treatments any way we can. My goal isn't so much the 'where' as the 'what.'"

And it wasn't an easy goal. Already he could tell that Layla was chastising herself for volunteering. She liked her creature comforts too much. And to think there'd been a time when he'd imagined they could work shoulder to shoulder here, that she wouldn't be bothered by the overall difficulty of pretty much everything. Well, he'd been wrong about that. Stars in his eyes. That's what he told himself afterward. Or maybe it had been the first time in his life he'd connected to a woman the way he had Layla.

Unfortunately, his situation doomed a relationship. But, if he were to pack up and leave for the sake of love, chances were nobody would come to take his place. The thought of letting down the people in his care made Arlo queasy and with that came the unrelenting knowledge that letting himself down was his course to follow. Forever alone. So, this is where he was, however it had happened. His choice, of course. And in that he'd been as stubborn or independent as he'd accused Layla of being.

"Your other option is to share my hut. It has a little more privacy—not much—but it's someplace where you can get away when you need to. Unless there's an emergency, people here know not to bother me when I'm in there." Arlo hadn't intended to ask her but now that he had, he didn't regret it.

When they had been together, they'd had fun evenings. Sitting, talking. Laughing. So maybe that was a bit of nostalgia creeping in. But those had been nice times and he didn't mind the reminders. Because once he and Layla had been very good together. Unfortunately, that had ended, but maybe having her here could shut the book on the bad and leave him with only the good. He hoped so as he didn't want to carry the weight of the bad with him for the rest of his life and, if he planned to spend that life alone, he wanted the good memories to look back on.

"You don't have to stand there looking so stressed, Arlo. I can do this job. Even more, I want to do this job."

"Because it's just another rung higher on your climb."

"Yes. I won't lie about that. Ollie needs team players in his surgery, and that's what I've been for quite a while now."

"Is it a struggle? Because I've never seen you as a team player. And I don't say that to offend you. But you always prided yourself on standing alone."

Layla laughed. "Because when you knew me,

that's all I'd ever done. Stood alone. So, it's always a struggle joining in, and I know that. So does Ollie. But this promotion means everything, so I've got a lot of work to do if I want to earn it. That demon of ambition is still there, Arlo, chipping away at me, and I thought something unexpected, like coming here, to the last place I thought I'd ever want to be, would help me learn what I need to know outside what I already know."

Arlo cocked his head and looked at her for a moment, then smiled. "I thought maybe he'd twisted your arm."

"You're the only one who ever tried to twist my arm and look how that turned out."

"I still can't believe you chose this, Layla. What were his other options?"

"Going to a sister hospital in Miami or working as assistant surgeon for a football team. Both short-term, fill-in positions like this. So, to be honest, I'm as surprised as you that I raised my hand for this. Especially since it scares me that I won't have what it takes to give your patients what they need. And you scare me, because—well, you fit here, and I don't." Layla bit down hard on her lip, and for a moment stared off into space.

"I—I don't want to fail, Arlo. I want to be the kind of person who can step into a situation—

any situation—and do what needs to be done. I mean, you've always known I have a huge fear of failure. And look at me now—marching into the center ring, pretty much without a clue. For me, this is really pushing the envelope, as they say. And while the whole you and me relationship thing is off the table, I need to be able to depend on you to help me, or at least point me in the right direction so I can figure it out myself.

"Even though being here and doing what I'm about to do scares me, I don't want to take the easy way out." Like giving in and going with him when she'd always known the life he led would make her miserable. Oh, she'd weighed the decision, for months. Made the mental pros and cons list. But in the end one thing had always tilted out of proportion to everything else—to be the best doctor she could be meant she had to be satisfied with her lifestyle.

What Arlo offered would never satisfy her. And, sure, maybe that was the leaning of the materialistic girl in her, but it was something that couldn't be overlooked. Layla had lost sleep over it, paced a rut in the carpet, bitten her nails to the quick, trying to figure out how to change herself, but, in the end, even her feelings for Arlo hadn't been strong enough to bring that about. Sadly, that was the answer. If she'd loved him enough, she should have been able to make the necessary changes in herself. But she couldn't, which meant she hadn't.

"Nope. You never were easy, and you never took the easy way out."

Arlo was decked out in tan cargo shorts and a faded navy blue T-shirt with the Voltaire saying on it: *The art of medicine consists of amusing the patient while nature cures the disease.* He looked like he belonged here. Layla was glad for him because she'd never really found that yet—a place where she belonged.

Working with Ollie in his hospital was good, and she liked it. But did she love it? She wanted to, but because there seemed to be such a long distance between like and love, she wondered if love could really exist—for what she did, or for the person she might spend her life with. The bottom line was she didn't know. Wasn't even sure she knew what love was.

"Maybe not being easy was some of my charm?"

"You had many charms, Layla. Trust me, you had more charm than you ever gave yourself credit for."

"You're just saying that because I was… convenient."

"You were a lot of things, but convenient was never one of them." He chuckled. "Even if I hadn't been raised in the jungle where I really didn't have much of an opportunity to get to know women, I'd have never called you convenient. Not in anything."

"Should I take that as a compliment?"

"There were many, many times I took it as a frustration. But it's who you were. Maybe still are. And, yes, it is a compliment because I did like your independence. It made you different from the others."

"Ah, yes. All the girls chasing after jungle boy. You did have your fair share, didn't you?"

"None who could hold my attention the way you did."

"Do you have someone now, Arlo? Are you married, or otherwise committed? I mean, I think Ollie might have told me, but you know how he is, the way he keeps as much to himself as possible. And I think he's gone out of his way not to mention you because, well—you know. It was awkward."

"There's no one. I did see someone in Bangkok for a while after I got back, but it didn't work out. She wanted attention all the time, and I didn't often have time to get there to give it to her. And she wouldn't come here. Eventually, she got to be very clingy, then demanding, when I refused an offer in one of the hospitals there. She'd set it up, assuming I'd take it but, well—you know me. You can take the jungle doc out of the jungle, but you can't take the jungle out of the jungle doc. I didn't conform enough for her and I certainly didn't want her to assume she could control me with a good job offer."

Arlo shook his head. "We lasted six long, difficult months then she met someone who could—and eventually did—give her all the things she wanted that I couldn't."

"I'm sorry to hear that."

"I'm not. She did much better than me. Besides, it's the story of my life. I can't bring anything to a relationship but me. I've got no money. Where I live—well, you'll see that for yourself. I don't own things. I work ridiculous hours. It wouldn't be fair of me to expect anybody to live that life, and it wasn't fair of me back then to ask you to, then end it the way I did, when you told me all the reasons you couldn't. At the time I was so…angry. Eventually I realized that anger was disappointment, and not in you. But in myself for expecting that I could ever have any kind of real relationship in my life since I have nothing to offer."

"You have yourself. If someone loves you, that should be enough."

"But that's not enough, Layla. You know it and I know it. But I made this choice, it was a promise to my mother. Now a lot of people depend on me. And if not me…there's nobody."

Layla shook her head as well. "I almost got myself into something once, but it's a long, complicated story. Girl on rebound meets wrong boy, mistakes his overtures for true love, boy tries to change girl to fit his mold, girl's not the type to bend into anybody's mold. In the end not a heartbreaker so much as an eye-opener and a huge caution that I'm better sticking to something where my heart doesn't get involved." And the last sentence of it went something like: Besides, he didn't measure up to Arlo. But Arlo didn't need to know that.

"Sorry to hear that. Even sorrier that I had a part in it."

She forced a sad smile to her face. "The truth is, I don't know what love is, Arlo. I recognize the kind my parents gave me—more obligatory love than the genuine thing. And don't get me wrong. They've spent a lifetime trying hard, not always getting it right, but trying. Which, I suppose, is love in some variation. At least the only way they knew how to give it. Then there's what I felt for you, which came with a time limit. I thought if I ignored it, it would magically disappear. Then Brad… I don't get it right, or don't do something right. Not sure which."

"Your parents you can't help. With me—us—the boundaries were there before we…" He swallowed hard. "Before we turned our friendship into something it wasn't meant to be. And with Brad, everybody makes that mistake sooner or later. The rebound affair. That's what I had with Gayle, I suppose. Someone to fill in the gaps."

"Then you were rebounding from me even though we weren't..."

"Readjusting," he said.

"I like that. And maybe that's what I was doing...readjusting." Readjusting to life after Arlo. Yet here she was, the one place she didn't belong given the feelings for him she'd had. But this time she was prepared. At least, she hoped she was. Because she needed to close this chapter. Even after all this time. "So, now that we know each other's biggest mistakes, how about showing me your hut?"

"Are you sure you'd actually stay with me after..."

"Just consider it like sleeping in on-call. Remember those days during our residency after long, hard hours where you barely had time to eat, let alone sleep, when any bed would do as long as the person occupying the bed next to you didn't snore?" She paused for a moment, and despite herself laughed. "You didn't start snoring, did you?"

"Haven't had any complaints. At least, on the nights when I sleep in the hospital, the patients

I'm watching haven't said anything. Neither has Chauncy."

"Who's Chauncy?"

Arlo chuckled. "You'll meet him soon enough. And probably get to sleep with him as well."

She didn't know what this was about, but his eyes were sparkling with laughter the way she remembered. It was nice seeing that again. Nice being part of it.

"No door?" she asked, as he pulled back the mosquito netting on his hut to let her in.

"Not yet. It's on the list of things I want, but the hospital gets the little funding we raise, not me, so it's not a priority."

A quick look revealed a small area where he prepared food, a desk off in one corner, a couple of rough-hewn chairs and a thin curtain separating a small area at the back from the rest of what was, essentially, a one-room hut. It was clear, and as basic a space as she'd ever seen, and she could picture Arlo living here. He'd always been a man of simple needs—something she'd admired about him. "So…no facilities?"

"Over at the hospital. Once you get used to it, it's not so bad."

"Bad, as in…?"

"Adequate. A hose through a window that brings water from a tank outside and takes a while to prime and get running. Or you can heat a bucket of water on the stove over there if you prefer a warm bath." He smiled. "I've lived in much more primitive digs than this so, to me, this is all good."

"Primitive for me was that weekend you took me to a cabin in the Catskills. Remember that?"

"It had indoor plumbing," he said defensively, smiling.

"And I had to carry in wood to the fireplace. In my life, a fireplace is turned on with a little knob off to the side. One little flick, gas turns on and, *voilà*, a fire." That had been a nice holiday, though. A wonderful holiday. No trappings like her parents required. Just simplicity and—the two of them. Snow outside, safe and warm with Arlo inside. Feeling protected by him. Drinking hot chocolate. Playing chess for hours on end. Making love for even more hours. Watching, through the plate-glass window, the snow coming down outside and being glad she was in Arlo's arms, inside. Perfect.

He chuckled. "I always did say you were a wimp."

"So, where's the switch to turn on your lights?" she asked, looking around for it.

"I have a generator, but fuel to run it's pretty expensive and hard to come by out here, so most of the time I light the place with a kerosene lamp. And candles. One of the women here makes candles for me."

While Ollie had tried to prepare Layla for Arlo's lifestyle, he hadn't come close. Yet she was here anyway. But it was only for two months, which did concern her—not the lack of amenities but being so close to Arlo because, already, memories she didn't want coming back were flooding in. The Catskills. Going to farmers' markets on the weekends. Reading out loud to each other at night—she liked Charles Dickens, he liked Stephen King. The way he'd always shown up at the hospital to walk her home when it was dark. Or check the oil and battery in her car, then go fill it up to make sure she wouldn't get stranded somewhere on the road. The big things…the little things. The things she'd taken for granted. So many of them were coming back to her now.

She'd expected some of that, but not so much, which made her wonder if what she'd thought of as a nice romance, or even an intense one at times, had really been much more. She knew she'd fallen in love with Arlo, but suddenly some of their memories were tearing at her heart. Even so, she didn't regret her decision to come to Thailand as there was a possibility she needed closure much more than she'd thought she did.

"And this is how you get along on a daily basis?" she asked, wondering if she could as well. Because she didn't want to embarrass herself in front of Arlo. There'd been too many times when he'd teased her about being a spoiled little rich girl, which had bothered her more than she'd expected it to. What she wanted more than anything was to show him she could do this on her own. Live this way. Be a good doctor. Be someone he respected. Because that's the one thing she'd never been sure she'd had from him—his respect. And now, even after all this time, she wanted it. Why? She didn't know. But it mattered. Mattered much more than she'd have ever guessed it would.

CHAPTER TWO

"SERIOUSLY? YOU CAN'T get antibiotics?"

Layla was reacting to a definite lack of supplies in Arlo's medicine lock-up. She'd taken a peek while she was over there and had been totally shocked. In comparison to what she'd had available to her all the time this was crazy. Yet it was Arlo's crazy, and he seemed good with it.

"I can, but it's not as easy as you'd think. Medical care is free, but I have to wait for my allotment, then it's sent to the regional hospital for me to pick up. Getting there isn't always easy. I don't always have time. And I can't have someone do it who isn't medically qualified."

"But don't you have an assistant?"

"He's a student, Layla. A college graduate who's getting ready to go to med school. And he's a good medic in the field. Trained by me, though. So he's not licensed or certified in any medical capacity yet, which means he can't make that trip. I have a nurse who'll bring my supplies out when he can, but doctors and nurses are in critically short supply outside the big cities, so he's not always free to help me either. Meaning if I need something immediately, sometimes I can go get it, sometimes I must wait, depending on what else is going on.

"Bottom line—what I need is available, but the ability to go after it is often lacking. So we wait, and make do until we can rectify the situation."

"I guess I never realized how difficult some medical situations can get, even when supplies are available."

"Most people don't. It's not their fault, but who wants to hear about what I do here when what's happening with medicine in Bangkok's hospitals is a huge contributor to the medical world in general. That's just the way it is."

In *her* medical world, a quick call to the pharmacy or central supply got her what she needed within minutes. Layla couldn't even begin to imagine the frustration of knowing you had what you needed available, yet you couldn't get to it. Maybe that was something she could fix. Something where her admin skills would prove to him she was good at what she did. Certainly it was worth looking into.

"So, can you stock ahead? Keep a few things back in case of emergency?"

"I do, but I don't have a lot of storage capacity here. And sometimes no electricity for days, which means the drugs that require refrigeration go bad."

It kept getting worse. No easy access to drugs that were his. Sometimes no ability to store them properly. And Arlo had chosen this over his grandfather's surgery? "Can't say that I understand any of this, Arlo. When you used to talk about coming back here, what you have isn't what you described. I pictured a modern facility tucked away in the jungle. Not a run-down structure that lacked supplies, personnel and anything that could be construed as convenient or up to date."

"But that's who we are. And this is what I knew I'd be getting when I came back."

"Do you have a bed?"

"Sure do. And it will be yours if you want it. Also, it's not a bed so much as a cot."

"And with the facilities across the street…"

"Consider it a little bit of rustic camping."

"For two months, Arlo. I can do that. But this is the rest of your life and even though I can see it, and I do have a better understanding of the need here…"

"Let me guess. You still don't get it?"

"Oh, I get it. But this isn't who you were when

we were together. You talked about this life, but you didn't live anything close to it."

"Consider that as me being on holiday."

"And I was part of that holiday?"

Arlo didn't answer the question. Instead, he pulled back a thin sheet separating the main part of the room from what looked to be a tiny space for a bedroom. "And you're in luck. Chauncy isn't here right now. So the cot is all yours if you want to rest until I can find someone to get your car."

Layla looked out the window above her cot and sighed. It was beginning to rain. Big fat drops. Hitting the dirt road and turning it into instant mud. And here she was, in a hut without a door, assigned to sleep with something or someone called Chauncy, and just now learning that what she'd thought might have been love in some form had been merely a holiday for Arlo. She'd been merely a holiday. Well, she was here. And she had to make the best of it while she was. But her spirits were as dreary as the gray sky outside. She'd hoped for something different, something more. And the truth hurt.

"I don't suppose this Chauncy happens to have an umbrella, does he? I'd like to go back across the road and get myself acquainted with the hospital."

"Actually, I have an umbrella. But you should

be careful because some snakes love the rain and come out to play, while others are making a mad dash to get out of it."

Yep, that's all she needed to add to her mood. Snakes in the puddles. "Seriously?"

"Seriously, but the good news is we have a nice supply of antivenin always handy. That's the one thing that's delivered to my door because the pharmaceutical reps deem my snakebite findings useful to them. So, use the antivenin, fill out some paperwork, answer some questions and they keep the supply coming."

Snakes *and* snakebites. Somehow none of this was brightening her day. Not this holiday girl.

"You trying to get rid of me already, Arlo?" Layla asked, walking into a small room, one of only three with real doors in the hospital, then stopping halfway inside to look around. It was a basic exam room. One hard, flat, old-fashioned exam table, an open cabinet with supplies like gloves, bandages and tongue depressors. The medicine cabinet she'd already seen. It wasn't great, but it wasn't hopeless either. More like something new in her collection of medical experiences.

"So, do you have a usual time to order supplies?"

"On a PRN basis." As needed.

"And you get that order sent by...?"

"Going to an elephant rescue near here and getting on their internet." Arlo smiled. "It may seem difficult, but it works out."

But would she work out inside Arlo's system? That was the question that kept coming to mind. She wanted to help him, to do a good job, but practically speaking, could she? "And I'll fit into this how?"

"Any way you want to. I operate on the same system as my orders are submitted. PRN. It works, as long as I don't get distracted. And that's when everything falls apart."

"What distracts you?" Layla was curious, as Arlo had never seemed the type to get distracted when they'd been together.

"A lot of things. Too much need, too little of me to go around. Medicines I can't get when I need them. The hole in the roof over my cot. Actually, now that you've displaced me that's one less distraction I'll have to deal with."

"Did you always feel that way about me, Arlo? That I distracted you?"

He gave her a questioning look. "How do you mean?"

"That I was a distraction you didn't want to have?"

"You were always a distraction, Layla. But

I wanted that distraction. Wanted that time we had together. It meant—everything."

To her, it had. But she wasn't sure about Arlo. One thing was certain, though. He'd been her distraction. And he'd displaced her feelings in a way no one would ever do again. Before him, she'd been sure what she wanted. But after him there had been times when she hadn't been so sure.

"Well, however it worked out, I'm glad you have everything you wanted," she said, walking out into the short corridor leading to the single room holding ten beds. All empty now. And everything bare bones. Meager. Medicine on a level she'd never seen. "Do you think Ollie might have provided you with more, had he known how bare your hospital is?"

"He knows, Layla. He's been here. But he's so heavily invested in his surgical practice—putting me through med school was enough. It was a very generous thing to do, especially considering that if he hadn't done it, I might still be struggling to earn enough money to get through. Besides, my parents were able to manage under difficult circumstances and so am I."

"I hope so. For your sake, as well as your patients'."

"You think I don't do what's best for my patients? You're here all of an hour and you're already making judgments?"

"Not at all. I'm beginning to realize how difficult it must be to exist here." She was almost gaining a deeper insight into him now, seeing him differently than she had in those years they had been together. And this side of Arlo was… admirable. He was someone to be respected. And it was so frightening, knowing he was out here, practically on his own, trying to make a difference she still didn't understand. "Since I've come a long way to work with you, I have the right to wonder. And worry, if that's the way it turns out. If that bothers you, sorry. But there's nothing I can do about it. At least, not until I understand more."

As Layla passed by Arlo on her way to the tiny kitchen at the rear of the ward, she paused when they were almost chest to chest and looked up at him. "I never worked directly with you when we were residents because of our personal situation. Fraternization wasn't allowed. But now it's different. And what we had, or what we meant to each other, can't get in the way. OK? The past is the past. So, keep in mind, Arlo, that this can't turn into something that's only about us. Taking offense too quickly at things not intended to be offensive, overreacting—we can't do that. We can't wipe the slate clean either. But we've got to find a way to make this work for a while. If that's what you want for your hospital. If it's not..."

She shrugged, then ducked into the tiny kitchen to assess the two-burner stove, the small utility table, and the knee-high refrigerator that looked to be a decade past its prime. It was working off a small generator that ran only the kitchen. Well, for now she'd have to get used to it. For better or worse, she had to make a go of this. And of Arlo.

For the first time, Layla really wondered why she had raised her hand so quickly. But it was too late to worry over that, especially when she had so many other things to fret about now. Snakes, something called Chauncy, rain, difficult conditions, Arlo... It was almost too much. Still, she was here, trying to convince herself she could do this. She had to. Arlo might suffer a little if she backed out, but his patients were the ones who really counted. Because of them, Layla would fight her way through and hope she was good enough. No matter what Arlo or anybody else thought, she was about being a doctor. A good doctor. As good a doctor as Arlo.

"What happened to your back?" Layla asked, as they both went to greet a patient who'd wandered in the door. A little boy with a scratch on his arm. He couldn't have been more than five or six, and Layla escorted the child to the exam room and pointed to the table, indicating for the child to hop up.

"I strained it a little," Arlo said, surprised and even flattered that she was paying that much attention. But Layla had always been observant. Sometimes too observant, especially when she'd picked up on one of his moods—moods he'd tried hard never to show. Yet she'd always known, just like now. "I fell off a roof. Actually, the roof caved in a little under my weight. That accounts for the hole over your cot." He said something to the child, who giggled with delight then made hand gestures to indicate someone falling. "Which is tarped, by the way. So the leak is only a drip."

"Should I ask what you were doing on a roof?" Layla found the antiseptic and scrubbed the child's wound, then dressed it with a bandage.

"Not unless you want to hear all about Chauncy."

"Ah, yes, my mysterious bed partner. So, why were you up on the roof with this Chauncy?"

"He got stuck. I had to help him down." Arlo dug into his cargo pockets and pulled out a sweet for the child, said something to him again, then sent the boy on his way, holding onto his sweet like it was the best prize in the world.

"Do children often come here alone?" Layla asked.

"The children here mature at an early age. Chanchai, the little boy who was just here, scratched his arm bringing in fishing nets."

"But he's only—"

"I know. By your standards you see a very young child. But by the standards here, he's a contributing member of the village and he has an important job. The twenty or thirty bahts here might only be a dollar or less in your currency, but that money goes to help support his family, making Chanchai's contribution very important."

"He's very…resilient."

"All the people here are. They work hard for their families, and even the young ones know to come to me if they're hurt, or not feeling well. Of course, it's easy to persuade them when they know you carry sweets in your pockets." He smiled. "Which isn't so different from anywhere, is it? I remember you during your pediatric rotation always stocking up candy for the children, even though your attending physician frowned on it."

"Because my doctor did that when I was a

child. It made the whole medical experience less frightening."

Arlo chuckled. "Remember that one little boy who'd follow you up and down the hall in his wheelchair, never saying a word but always giving you that sad look when you gave a sweet to another child?"

"Geordie. I haven't thought of him in years. He did manage to finagle his fair share, didn't he?"

"Because you were a pushover when it came to children. It surprised me that you went into general surgery and not pediatrics. You were so good with the kids."

"Pediatrics broke my heart too often. I— um— To be an effective doctor I needed to be more detached."

For someone who tried so hard to be stone-hearted, he'd seen through the façade to a very soft, caring woman. It had shone in Layla's face every time she'd looked at one of her pediatric patients. She couldn't hide it—at least, not from him. "Well, you would have been good at it, and you will get your fair share of children to treat here."

"Hope I'm up to it better than you were up to your climb on the roof with Chauncy. Who is…?"

Arlo put the antiseptic and bandages back in

the cabinet, looked out the window and spun around to face her.

"He's actually just come home. Want to come meet him?"

He waved at Samron, an aged widow who spent several hours each day in Happy Hospital, cleaning, doing laundry, serving meals and other jobs that gave her something to keep her busy. She was also the self-appointed receptionist who greeted patients when they came in.

"I'll be across the street if you need me," he said to her.

Yes," she answered, smiling. "With pretty lady doc. Your wife?"

Arlo chuckled, then explained to Layla. "They all want me to settle down, get married, start a family. I'm usually on the receiving end of a fix-up at least twice a month. Somebody's sister, or cousin, or daughter."

"Sounds like they care about you."

"Maybe a little too much." He smiled at Samron and shook his head. "Not wife. New lady doc. Doc Layla."

Samron nodded, but her smile told the story, and it was all about Arlo and Layla, together. "Doc Layla," she repeated, then pressed the palms of her hands together in a prayer-like fashion, bent her head ever so slightly and said, "*Wai*," a customary Thai greeting.

Layla did the same, then followed Arlo into the road. "She seems very nice," she said.

"And very helpful. She also volunteers at the school. And on the weekends she spends time with new mothers in the village, helping them with their babies. She's a very respected person here."

"Respect is important," Layla said. "Too many people have forgotten what it is."

"Well, it's not like that here. If you earn respect, you're given respect." Arlo entered his hut and went straight to the curtain separating the room into two. Then pulled it back to reveal…

"What is that?" Layla asked, her eyes wide open.

"This is Chauncy, my civet cat. We co-habit."

"A civet cat is…?"

"Something like a cat, only a little larger with a face kind of like a big rat. They're nocturnal so they have really glowy eyes."

"And your civet cat got stuck up on the roof and when you went to get him you fell through? Couldn't he have come down himself? I'm assuming civet cats can climb. You know, the law of jungle survival and all that."

"They can, but Chauncy's not good at it. He had a broken leg when I found him, and it healed leaving him lame. So he can climb up pretty well, but getting down is the problem."

"And now he's your house cat?"

"Pretty much." Arlo smiled. "You'll get used to him."

Layla took a couple steps closer, then stared down at the creature who didn't resemble a cat, curled up on the cot she would use. "He's clean, I suppose," she said, bending down to pet him. "And he doesn't bite?"

"Very clean. He doesn't really wander out in the jungle anymore. He's pretty domesticated, and since the people here all know him, they feed him, which makes him too fat, which also makes him lazy. And, no, he doesn't bite. Also, his scent gland was removed since he had to be domesticated for his survival, so you're safe there as well."

She bent to pet Chauncy, who raised his head long enough to decide she was no threat, then immediately went back to sleep. "He's… beautiful," she said, speaking in a whisper so she didn't disturb him.

"I recall you liked cats." Arlo had been concerned that living with a wild animal might cause Layla problems since she was strictly big city but watching her relate to Chauncy gave him a whole new appreciation for her. In fact, he admired the way she simply accepted the fact that she'd be curling up with a jungle creature.

That wasn't the Layla he remembered. She'd been…highly strung.

"Cats, dogs, civet cats. All God's creatures, Arlo. Just didn't expect to be sleeping with one. But when you're in the jungle I suppose you sleep with the civet cats when you must." She tiptoed away from Chauncy then moved to the opposite side of the cottage. "Just no snakes," she said. "They're free to roam around all they want outside the hut, but not inside, please."

Arlo laughed. He'd always liked her practicality. When other female med students had been trying to attract him by flirting or making offers that hadn't interested him, Layla had been the one who hadn't noticed him. Which had made him want her to.

And he'd worked hard to get her attention, finding out afterward, when they were together, that's what she'd wanted all along. But she'd been so inexperienced—not shy, though—as much as reserved. Like she had been testing the water and he had been the water. But it had been cute watching her find her way in their relationship. Even after that night with the popcorn, there had been so many things she hadn't known. Things he'd delighted in showing her. Simple things like hiking in the woods. Complicated things such as the profound pleasure an uncomplicated massage could offer.

She'd led a sheltered life, though. Hadn't ever really had anyone there to guide her. She also hadn't had to contend with civet cats, snakes and elephants daily, the way he'd done, growing up. Talk about opposites… Honestly, he'd always been a little protective of that side of her. Now he wondered if it still existed, and if it did, would it bring that out in him again? "Snakes have their place. If you know which ones won't kill you."

"Good information to have handy," Layla said in the matter-of-fact tone Arlo remembered, oh, so well, as she sat cross-legged on the floor near the door and patted the floor next to her. It was a tone that meant she was trying to stay aloof, trying to avoid contact, commitment or whatever else frightened her. Understandably, she was probably more frightened of him right now than snakes. Yet here she was, trying to face it. That was a new side of her, one he liked a lot.

"So, since we don't have proper facilities in here, I suppose buying a luxurious spa tub with soothing jets and all kinds of bubble bath is out of the question? As well as a heated towel rack?"

Arlo laughed as he sat down "Afraid so, but we've got a stream about half a mile from here where the water's pretty warm this time of year. And if the temperature's hot enough, the rocks heat up so you can consider that your heated towel rack."

"You always kept me amused, Arlo. I remember some of those long nights of studying after a long day of working in the hospital, when I thought I wasn't cut out to be a doctor. Then there you'd be, cooking me some of the worst food I'd ever eaten, or strumming your guitar and making up songs that didn't make sense."

"They were in Thai," he defended.

"No, they were in gibberish. Even I recognized that. And if I hadn't, the look on your face would have given you away."

"There were good times, weren't there?" Arlo asked, twisting his back to find a comfortable position.

"And bad ones. I just wish we'd had the bad ones at the beginning so when we finally decided to call it quits we'd have had the good ones closest to us. It would have made the memories better, I think."

He had good memories of her and that was the problem. The memories were too good for a couple that was destined to break up. "And here we are, together again."

"But not for that reason," Layla warned. "I really do want to prove myself and working here should earn me some..."

"Some what?" he asked.

She shook her head. "Has your cooking gotten any better?" she asked, deliberately changing the subject.

"Actually, my brother Eric—you remember me talking about him, don't you?"

"The rich one."

"One and the same. Anyway, he sent me a yakitori grill. And while I'm not good at preparing a meal on it, I do make a mean cup of tea."

"A yakitori grill? Does that mean you've been to Japan?"

"No, my brother lives there. He sent it to me. But I haven't had time to visit him yet."

"So, you've got a civet cat *and* a yakitori." She reached out and squeezed Arlo's arm—an affectionate gesture from the past that came so naturally.

"That about sums it up."

"And that makes you a happy man?"

"Along with my practice. You know me. Simple needs."

"And mine weren't, were they?"

"Let's just say that you gravitated more toward the finer things in life. Probably still do, for all I know."

Layla sighed. "To be honest, I don't have time for all the finer things in life. Most of my time is spent working."

"Why am I not surprised?"

"Probably because you always knew I was ambitious. I think I probably slammed that in your face a thousand times in those two years, didn't I?"

He chuckled. "Let's just say that I was well aware of your preferences and leave it at that."

"Was I that bad, Arlo?"

"You were never bad, Layla. Neither was I. But as a couple…well, our destinies precluded everything else. Maybe that's what was bad. That, and those fifty pairs of shoes on the closet floor that left me no room for my two pairs."

He smiled, thinking about how he'd practically lived out of a suitcase during those two years because her clothes had taken up every inch of hanging space in both bedrooms. But that had been part of her charm. At least, to him it had been, because he'd loved watching her make the decision of what to wear.

It would take hours sometimes, and she'd always asked his opinion. *Do you like me in this? Is this one better than the other one?* It always made him feel a part of something other than the jungle or his parents' life. Something he liked, even though it was temporary.

"Never more than forty, Arlo. Unless you count boots."

He laughed out loud. Couldn't help himself. Even though they weren't a couple, something about the old familiarity was sinking back in, making him feel like, well—what he hadn't felt like since they had been a couple. "Well, no worries about that here, since this hut doesn't have a closet."

"To think this is where you expected me to live. And that was back when I only had thirty pairs of shoes."

"Sixty," he teased.

"We'll compromise at twenty," she said, smiling.

"Well, for what it's worth, I never expected you to take me up on my offer. But in a few of my more stupid moments, I did hope."

"Not stupid, Arlo. Hope is never stupid."

"Except when it came to us."

Layla smiled, but it was tinged with sadness. "So, is a hose for a shower and no closets what you still want? I know you feel an obligation to stay here, but has anything changed?"

"No, not really. Because this is where I've always worked from the time I was five or six, just like little Chanchai. It's everything I knew I wanted, probably because this is the kind of medicine my parents practiced, and I respected what they did. I mean, I was raised in the jungle, Layla. Conceived here, born here. It's what I know. What I want. Taking care of people who wouldn't otherwise get medical help—I could have gone in with Ollie after I graduated, but it wouldn't have made me happy, not the way my practice here does."

"Then you're where you belong. Following your heart is always the best way."

"Have you ever done that, Layla? Followed your heart?"

She shook her head. "That's not who I am. I follow my choices, but you already knew that."

"I hope your choices have made you happy so far."

"They've made me what I want to be—successful."

And somehow Layla seemed almost as vulnerable as she had when they'd first been together. The girl who'd been afraid to approach him. The girl who'd never fully invested herself in life. Was it because of her money? Did she still rely on that the way she had when they'd been together? Trusting that rather than trusting people?

There'd been so many times when she'd found it easier to buy her way into a situation rather than rely on her intellect and amazing abilities to come up with a better way. Was that who she still was? Because that was a part of Layla he'd never understood. So independent, yet so willing to fall back into habits she'd said she wanted to be rid of. Even if they hadn't been going in separate directions, that's the thing that would have killed them.

"I suppose I thought that after you'd spent so much time back in the States during medical school, then residency, maybe this wouldn't have the same appeal you remembered."

"It has more, now that I'm an adult and can fully appreciate what I have here—like the freedom of doing what I want to do without a lot of interference from anyone. My patients are the best, which makes up for my less than spectacular accommodation. And it's nice caring for people who are grateful for my services and not ones who make unreasonable demands."

He laughed. "Remember the surgical patient who wanted me to do both a hernia repair and a nose reduction in the same surgery? The guy actually reported me to Administration because I refused, not that my attending would have allowed such a thing even if I'd wanted to. Which I didn't. But he made my life miserable for a couple of weeks, calling and complaining over and over."

"If I recall, he thought he'd get a discount that way. Two surgeries for the price of one anesthesia. Guess he didn't consider that general surgeons aren't plastic surgeons. Or maybe that didn't matter to him. You were pretty agitated at the time."

"And you made me chicken noodle soup—from a can."

"Because it was supposed to make you feel better."

"When you were ailing, Layla. I wasn't ailing. I was angry." He smiled. "But it was a nice gesture, having someone take care of me like that. Did I ever tell you how much I appreciated that?"

"No. You told me it wasn't hot enough, then told me to reheat it in the microwave. But you did leave me that flower the next day—the one you picked from the garden at our apartment building. I pressed it and kept it until, well—I probably still have it tucked in a book somewhere. It was the first gift you ever gave me." Layla smiled, and leaned her head over on his shoulder, a natural thing she'd always done once upon a time. "I'm glad it's working for you, Arlo."

"I…um…" Arlo pulled away from her so quickly she almost fell sideways to the ground. "We've got work to do," he said, his voice suddenly stiff.

"Did I do something?" she asked, trying to recover from his abruptness.

Arlo shook his head as he stood. "We did something a long time ago and I don't want to repeat it. You're not easy to resist, Layla. God knows, I was never able to. But not anymore. My work—my practice here won't allow me that kind of distraction."

"That's right. I was just your holiday girl, wasn't I? Well, don't worry. I'm nobody's holiday now, and I never will be again." Without another word, Layla marched out of the hut and across the road to the hospital, grabbed the schedule off the desk at the front and saw that the next three patients due in needed general care—a wound check, an antibiotic shot and a maternity appointment. They weren't there yet, but when they arrived they would find Dr. Layla Morrison waiting for them in the exam.

And Dr. Arlo Benedict standing outside in the road, in the rain, wondering how two people who'd gotten it so right could have also gotten it so wrong.

CHAPTER THREE

IT WAS GETTING ON in the day when Layla finally gathered up the courage to go back to the hut to face him. Overall, seven patients had come to the hospital and she'd managed to figure out what each one wanted. Luck had been with her on that one. That, plus some translation help from Samron, who seemed genuinely pleased to be useful.

"Have you eaten yet?" she asked Arlo, who was heading back to the hut at the same time she was.

"A couple of times. My house call patients always like to offer food." He handed her a wooden plate covered with a cloth napkin. "Khao pad. It's a fried rice with several different vegetables and pork in it. There's also some mixed fruit."

"I, um—I don't know what to say except thank you and I'm sorry. This is awkward and I know it, and I shouldn't have gotten so familiar. Leaning against you that way was inappropriate, but just for a few minutes we were almost—us. The way we started anyway. From now on I'll keep my distance."

"And I never meant to imply you were a holiday girl. You were my break from reality, and you knew that. But I never thought of you as someone who was there only for a good time, someone to use at my convenience, and I'm sorry that's how it sounded."

"I know who we were, Arlo. From the very first day until the last one, I always knew. I also know that's not what you thought of me but, like I said, it's awkward now." She peeked at the food under the cloth, and her mouth practically watered. "Mind if I heat this up on your yakitori?"

"Communal property while you're here, Layla. What's mine is yours."

"So, where do I put my fifty pairs of shoes?"

He laughed as they went inside together, she straight to the yakitori, to lay the fire beneath it, and he to his mat on the floor. But when he lowered himself to it, he winced.

"I really do need to have a look at that," she said, pulling a matchbox from a shelf and lighting the fire. "Even if I can't see anything, maybe I can feel which muscle is giving you problems and manipulate some of that soreness out of it.

Strictly medical, of course." She turned around and studied him for a moment. It wasn't quite dark in the hut yet, but it wasn't quite light either. Yet somewhere in the ebbing of the day she saw traces of the man who'd shared her bed for nearly two years mingling with traces of a man she didn't know.

"You've changed," Layla said, not caring that he could see her assess him. His hands—yes, she was a handsy type. Always looked at the hands second. Neck first. Eyes. Mouth. But right now she was wondering if his hands would still be soft. They looked soft, and she wondered what they would feel like on her skin again. Caressing her. Causing her to tingle…

No, this wasn't allowed. No memories. No fond thoughts of what they'd had. Still, Arlo Benedict, for his un-trendy ways, was a rugged and well-proportioned man. A head-turner. Always had been, and she was pretty sure he'd never even been aware of it.

"How?" he asked. "And if it's in a bad way, please lie to me. I know the jungle can be harsh."

"Quite the contrary. You look…more mature. Not so much in the physical sense as what I can see in your eyes."

"I think that's called wisdom. Before I went to medical school I was here with my parents, working as their helper. They had everything under control and that's what I expected to come back to. But when I did come back, my mother was gone, and my dad wasn't the same. He stayed around long enough to help me find my way, then he went to live his own life, leaving me here with a lot of expectations that weren't mine to have. I expected what my parents had but my reality was that I had to build my own place here, gain trust that was mine and not my parents'. So I wised up pretty fast. Had to in order to survive."

"Well, it looks good on you." Layla turned back to the yakitori, pulled a metal pot off the shelf above it and dumped in her fried rice. While it heated, she ate large chunks of papaya and mango with her fingers.

"You've changed, too," Arlo said, still wrestling to find a comfortable position. "You used to be…reserved. Or at least not as sure of yourself. You grew out of that a little while we were together but now you're this dynamic ball of fire that plows through everything. Instead of talking about what you wanted to happen, you're making things happen in your life, and I'm glad it's working out for you."

She pulled the rice off the little stove then turned back to face him. "Care to share?" she asked, thinking of the many times they'd ordered one meal and shared it, both eating from the same plate. Sometimes feeding each other. Often with just fingers. So nice. Sensual. So much intimacy in such a simple gesture.

Patting his flat belly, Arlo shook his head. “When I make evening calls, I have to pace myself with what I eat because everybody wants to cook for me.”

“And I usually grab something from the hospital before I leave for the evening.” She wrinkled her nose. “Haven’t learned to cook properly yet.”

“Well, I didn’t move in with you because you were a domestic goddess. And I did know that you sneaked in a maid to do the cleaning.”

“Seriously?” And she’d thought she’d been so stealthy about it.

“Remember that vacuum we bought? You didn’t even know how to turn it on. It was a flip switch. On and off. And you didn’t know how. Yet the apartment was always spotless.” He laughed so hard it caused a spasm in his back. “I let you keep your secret because you were trying so hard to be domestic that I didn’t want you to know I was well aware of the *real* you.”

“Only once a week,” she said, taking her plate of rice across the room and sitting down across from Arlo. At a safe distance. So there was no way to lean, or touch, or even accidentally brush up against him. "And I really thought you didn't catch on."

"Oh, I caught on. But it was…cute, how you'd try to hide things. Like more shoes, when you bought them. I was always wise to you, Layla."

"But I was never wise to you. So, how did that happen?"

"I think we see what we want to see. Or we don't see what we don't want to see. I don't think you wanted to see the real me."

"Yet you wanted to see the real me."

"Because there was so much to see. So many facets." He smiled. "And secrets."

"Secrets? Besides the shoes and the maid, and the takeaway food. Oh, and the laundry…"

"You had someone do the laundry?"

She nodded, watching his face for a reaction. Which happened immediately in a broad smile and a loud laugh. "Are you kidding me? Because I never knew that."

"I didn't want you thinking I was too incompetent. But I didn't know how to sort laundry or even turn on a machine."

"So, who?"

"The woman who worked for my mother. She'd stop by a couple times a week, grab what needed to be cleaned and leave what she'd already done. So, is there a secret behind those sandals?" She referred to the well-worn pair sitting on the shelf outside the door. "Because I don't see another pair of shoes in here." Traditionally, shoes were left outside on a rack, and houses were entered either barefoot or in socks. It was interesting that Arlo respected tradition enough to do that in his own hut, where he wouldn't have to if he didn't want to. It was a nice quality, paying homage to a tradition that wasn't his. Yet he fit this place so well. Much better than any place she'd ever tried to fit. She envied him that as it was something she doubted she'd ever have.

"Until I can afford a new pair, it's them or nothing."

"And I'm betting that once you have enough money for a new pair, you put that money to what you would consider a better use." Arlo was like that. Always taking care of others before he took care of himself. Even when they'd been together and Layla had been struggling through a particularly difficult lesson in physiology or couldn't quite remember the function of every bone in the body, he'd stop his studying to help her through hers.

There were so many little details she'd taken for granted then, which were coming back to her now. To think she'd had so much yet couldn't hold onto it. And maybe, in some ways, she'd pushed it away, knowing she came in second to his dream—a dream that would never include her.

"I might," he confessed. "But the soles are still intact, the straps keep them on me, and with a little tape I'm good for now. Besides, I don't have a closet, so where would I put them since you've got, what? Ten pairs lined up against the wall?" He tossed her a sexy wink.

There was something to be said for a doctor who devoted everything he had to his practice. She did admire that. Much more now that she could see it than before, when it had been mere words. And while none of this was for her in the long term, she was anxious to see how it worked. To see how Arlo worked. For his sake, she hoped everything was good for him because, despite their rocky time at the end, she did want him to be happy with his choice, even though his choice didn't include her.

"You don't happen to still have some of those socks I bought you, do you? They'd look stunning with your sandals."

She smiled, thinking of all the outrageous socks and underpants she'd bought him over the course of their relationship, trying to loosen him up a bit. Not that he was stodgy. But he was a man of habit. Everything was the same—all his socks alike, the same with his underpants. So every now and then she'd thrown in something a little different and hidden one of his tried-and-trues.

At first, it had simply been colors. Red socks, plaid socks. Then figures—pickles, kittens. Santas for Christmas. Hearts for Valentine's Day. Eventually came the unicorn socks, underpants and T-shirts. And that was when he'd finally commented. Actually, his comment had been to balk at wearing them, but by the time the unicorns had arrived he'd had no choice but to wear what she'd bought as she'd hidden everything else.

"Ah, yes. The unicorns. Those got dumped in the trash shortly after I left."

"But you wore them."

"Did I have a choice? You took away everything else. And did I ever tell you how badly I was ridiculed in the locker room at the hospital when I changed into my scrubs?"

"You never said a word, but I heard."

"Everybody heard, and I was so..."

"Cute. Maybe even a little bit sexy."

"In unicorns? I was going to say I was so humiliated."

"Yeah, but remember the night you came home and paraded those unicorns around the—" This was going too far. The memories were of something she shouldn't be remembering. Yet being around Arlo seemed to knock down all her defenses—defenses she'd struggled to raise in the few days she'd had between knowing she was coming here until arriving. "You know what? Instead of tea, I think I'd like to go back over to the hospital to make sure I've replaced everything I used today."

"You can't run from it, Layla. We have history, and considering what we were together I'm not sure you should have come."

She pushed herself off the floor and took the plate over to the bucket that was used for washing dishes. "I'm not denying what we had, Arlo. And you're not the reason I'm here. I want that promotion and I thought that if Ollie saw how well I could function under adversity, that would put me one step closer."

"Is the jungle the real adversity here, or am I?"

She didn't answer him, because she didn't know what to say. So maybe she'd deluded herself into believing that Arlo wouldn't be a factor in her goals. Or maybe she'd simply hoped he wouldn't. Whatever the case, he was an obstacle and she was going to have to be very careful. Because in the span of only one day a new truth about the way she'd felt about Arlo was trying to force itself in. And it was a truth she didn't want to admit was there.

* * *

It was interesting, getting to *again* know someone he'd shared a bed with for two years. In many ways she was still the same, yet in as many ways she was different. She'd never really asked questions about how he'd live his life here when they'd been together. Mostly, she'd assumed what it would be, and had let that play on the way she accepted things. Now, watching her face his reality, she wasn't overwhelmed the way she might have been years ago. Curious, yes. Even ready to be involved. But she was looking at things differently. Even seeing him differently. Of course, he was seeing her differently as well. Time and maturity, he supposed. And also a good dose of their own, personal realities.

"Tell me about Eric," she said, from the other side of the curtain.

It was late, but he wasn't ready to sleep. Neither was she, as he'd been listening to her over there for the past hour, settling in, making adjustments, arranging her belongings. Getting her cot well away from the drippy ceiling so she wouldn't feel the splash as the leaking water hit the bucket. As he recalled, she'd never been the first to go to sleep. She was more of a polyphasic sleeper—sleeping in bursts, napping in between—while he was a hunker down and get to sleep as fast as he could kind of guy. He remembered the many nights when he'd waken briefly to find her simply staring at him. It was nice, knowing she watched him sleep.

"He's got a good life going. Married, has a son. Living in Japan."

"Did he ever get to see your mom before she—?"

"He did. It was difficult for both of them, especially with the way she left him when he was so young."

"And you didn't even know you had a brother until you were, what? Twenty?"

"Almost twenty-one."

"I never knew how something like that could happen. I always wanted a brother or sister because I was so alone growing up. If I'd found out, only after I was an adult, that I had a brother or sister, I don't know that I could have forgiven my parents." She poked her head around the curtain. "Yet you've always seemed very calm about that."

"Because I was."

"But not Eric?"

"He had a lot of resentment, even after he knew the reason our mother walked away. I think being a married man with a family of his own has made it better for him. And I can't even begin to understand what it would be like having a mother who walked away from me. But that's what our mother did."

"And you don't resent her for keeping her secret?"

"What I resent was that Eric's dad put her in the position that forced her to keep secrets from her sons. I don't blame her for what she did, and in time I don't think Eric will either."

"But the good news is you have a brother."

"And the relationship between us is getting better. Can't say that it's great yet. Especially since we live in two totally different worlds. But it's nice knowing he's out there."

"So, did your mother ever tell you why? Or am I getting too personal?"

"It's personal, but you lived through some of the ups and downs of it, so you have a right to know."

She came around the curtain, with her hair up in a ponytail the ways she'd always put it up at night, but instead of the cute nightwear she used to wear—short shorts, barely there belly shirts—she was wearing knee-length cargo pants, a baggy T-shirt and boots. Still cute, in its own special way.

"She tried legally for partial custody, but Eric's father wanted his legacy and my mother was only the means by which he could get what he wanted. After he had his son, he didn't need her, so he kicked her out. Then after she tried to maintain a place in Eric's life—let's just say that in my own dad's earlier days he wasn't a saint. He smoked some weed, was arrested a couple of times—although he has no convictions.

"But Eric's dad found out and used that to threaten my mother—told her he'd expose her husband, my dad, and by that time she'd had me and he also said he'd expose her as an unfit mother for allowing me to be raised by a man like my dad. Things were different back then. My mother was afraid of losing me, and afraid my dad could lose his medical license, even though there were never any real charges brought against him. Eric's dad had a lot of power and he wasn't afraid to use it. Also, because she'd been so abused by Eric's dad to begin with, she simply didn't have the wherewithal to fight him.

"So, because she feared losing both my dad and me, after she'd already lost Eric, she walked away." He paused, then sighed. It was a sad sigh that resounded loudly through the hut, filling it with the same sadness. "My mother wasn't a fighter, Layla. She was a very quiet, undemanding person. And after all she'd already suffered..."

"I'm so sorry," Layla whispered. "You didn't know this when we were—?"

He shook his head. "My dad only told me the whole story a couple years ago. He kept my mother's secret for a long time, then finally decided it was time I knew everything."

"And you told Eric?"

"He had a right to know. He was settling into his new life and I knew he harbored a lot of resentment for our mother, but because his son was our mother's grandchild, I thought for Riku's sake—that's his name—everybody needed to know the truth. And I did want my nephew to know how amazing his grandmother was. She was part of his heritage and he deserves to know the good about her. Eric didn't want to know, but for the sake of his son I had to tell him."

"I wish I'd known. Wish I could have helped you. Some things are so difficult when you're alone. I really am sorry for that."

"Well, the good news is Eric now has memories of a mother he can be proud of, and Riku has a grandmother who would have loved him more than life itself. He'll understand that when he's old enough. Eric will make sure."

Layla wiped a tear siding down her cheek. "And your father?"

"In Cambodia. Doing well. Running a little clinic in a tourist area."

"And I thought I had it bad because while I had my parents' time, I never really had their love. At least, love in the sense that I think parents should have for their children."

"Maybe they did the best they could, the way my mother did."

"They do," she admitted. "But that understanding comes as an adult, not as a child who was simply lonely. Anyway, I'm going to get some sleep. It's been a long, full day and since Chauncy has vacated my bed now, I think it's time."

This time, Arlo lay awake long after Layla was asleep, thinking back on the day. This morning, he'd known someone was coming. Hadn't known who but wasn't surprised as Ollie would have sent him only the best. And Layla was the best. It concerned him she was here, but he was also looking forward to the next couple of months with her. No deluding himself about anything, though. She was still Layla, and Layla didn't belong here. On top of that, she didn't want to belong here. But over the course of the years there'd been many, many times when he'd wondered what it would be like, having Layla at his side.

Well, for a little while he had that chance, and he was glad about that. What he wasn't glad about were the feelings that would hit him again once she'd gone. He'd been through that and had been nearly crippled by emotions he'd never expected. It wasn't until he'd left her that he'd truly realized how much he'd loved her. This time he was smarter. No hearts involved meant no hearts broken. And she was clear that her heart was in her career and nowhere ese. But his? Where was it?

"Damn," he muttered, as he blew out the kerosene lamp and turned over on his side. Winced because of his back. Then turned again.

"I really do need to look at that," she said from the other side of the curtain. "Tomorrow. I'll pencil you in as my first appointment of the day."

He smiled. She never gave up. That may have been one of the things he'd loved most about her back then. But now?

"Baby's on the way…"

Layla didn't open her eyes when Arlo's voice wafted over her. It was a dream. They were cozy in their apartment, cuddled up, studying. Maybe some playing mixed in. And he was explaining…

"Contractions just a couple of minutes apart, Layla."

"Dilated?" she asked, her mind still all snuggly on a sofa back in New York.

"Has been since yesterday, when I checked her."

She loved his voice when it was all serious. It was deeper, sexier. "Epidural, I'm assuming," she said.

"We don't do epidural out here."

"Better call anesthesia." He should have already done that. She didn't understand why he hadn't.

"Do you want to come with me, Layla?"

"Where?" she asked, her eyes still closed.

"To deliver a baby."

This time her eyes shot open and she realized where she was. Not in Arlo's arms, studying the basics of childbirth, but in a jungle hut with a patient who was ready to deliver. She bolted upright. "Who's with her?" she asked, sliding off the cot and running over to the door to grab her boots.

"Empty them first," Arlo warned. "I can't handle a delivery and a snakebite at the same time."

Reality. This was her reality for a while. She shook the dream away totally as vigorously as she shook her boots. "How long has she been in labor?"

"Off and on since yesterday. I checked her earlier, when I was making rounds, and contractions were still about ten minutes apart. But it seemed to have sped up."

"How long have I been sleeping?" she asked.

The fact was her sleeping was so erratic, she often didn't know.

"About two hours."

"And you've been working..."

"About the same."

Layla grabbed her medical rucksack and rushed out the door. Arlo followed, amused by the way she went from sound asleep to at the ready. She'd always been a little bit difficult to wake, but once he'd succeeded she'd been on the spot, bright-eyed and ready to go. "Her mother's with her. And her grandmother. Also, there's a midwife, and she'll do most of the work."

"So what will we do?" she asked.

"Respect the traditions. I just thought you might want to see how this works, since we've got at least a dozen more pregnant women in the village and you'll no doubt be called to watch but not participate in the birth unless there's a problem."

"I know a lot of places in the world don't welcome outside interference. Is this one of them?"

"No. They love having a hospital. It's the only one around for nearly a hundred miles, so they take pride in having medical services here. But they also have their traditions, which I don't interfere with unless they become a problem." He pointed to a well-apportioned hut, one with a door, at the end of the road. "It's bigger than yours," she said, following him up the path to the front door.

"Because I don't have my parents, grandparents and children living with me. Family is a large part of their tradition."

Which she saw for herself when she and Arlo went inside. There were women cooking, children playing, men talking. And in the doorway to the area where the bedrooms probably were stood an old woman holding a tiny bundle in her hands. "I see they didn't really need us," Layla said, pushing her way through the crowd to look at the newborn. The old woman, named Hanni, immediately put the baby in Layla's arms then headed off to the area where the food was being prepared. In her medical practice Layla didn't deal with children and, in all honesty, she hadn't even handled one since her rotation through Pediatrics during her residency. And this one—he was so tiny. Red, wrinkled and screaming for all he was worth.

"They named him Arlo," Arlo said, stepping to her side.

"Even though you didn't deliver him?"

"It's a tribute."

"So, how many little Arlos are running around the village?"

"At last count, five. This Arlo makes number six."

"Well, if ever there was a village legacy..." Layla grinned, reaching down to take baby Arlo's tiny fingers. "Suppose you have a son someday and want to call him Arlo? What then?"

"Just accept the fact that he'll be one of the many." He pulled back the blanket to have a better look at the baby. "You look good with a baby. Ever thought that maybe you might...?"

"I haven't changed on that," she said. "I told you back then I didn't want children, and I still don't. I'm the living proof of how badly it can work out when the parents are all about career, and I'd never want that for my child because, in my family, the apple doesn't fall far from the tree, even though the career tree is different." She handed the baby over to him. "Think I'll go look in on the mother to make sure she's getting along OK." And to get away from the cozy feeling of home and family that was coming over her.

"I've got another house call to make after this," he called after her. She heard him but didn't respond as she ducked out of the room and found an empty room down the hall where she could hide long enough to gather her wits. And will her hands to stop shaking. Of everything that was going to be difficult here, this might be the worst. Because she'd had these thoughts before. Although she'd never told

Arlo. What was the point when their directions were so vastly different?

It was mid-afternoon when they caught up again. Layla had taken the hospital calls while Arlo had done rounds in the village.

It was nice having her here to help him. While his assistant was good, he wasn't a doctor so his duties were limited. But having two doctors here—the way his parents had been—would be nice. Even after only a day and a half, he was getting spoiled by it.

But not spoiled enough to let himself believe the other doctor would be Layla. Because, as they said, a leopard didn't change its spots. Neither did Layla. One look at the baby and the almost panicked expression on her face had said it all.

"I've got a house call to make. It's out some way, so I thought you'd like to go with me to see some of the countryside. And if you don't, could I borrow your SUV?"

They were both back in the hut, getting tidied up for the rest of the day. When Arlo peeked around the dividing curtain to talk to her, he had to bite his lower lip to keep from laughing. Chauncy had managed to find his way onto Layla's lap, and she was simply sitting cross-legged on the cot, petting him. Normally, he wasn't quite so friendly with strangers, but Layla did have a way about her. Especially considering that Chauncy wouldn't even cuddle up to him that way.

Somehow, seeing a gray, ring-tailed raccoon-looking mongoose-rat creature all cozy with her caused a lump to form in his throat. This was the other side of her, one he'd loved as much as he'd loved her harder side. There'd been times when she'd just snuggle into him for no reason and simply exist in his embrace. No kidding, no anything else. Just touch. Sensation. And he'd enjoyed those moments as they'd felt so caring. So consuming.

"What do we have?" she asked, plucking a quartered mango from a bowl next to her and handing it to Chauncy.

As the juice dribbled down her arm, Arlo could almost imagine himself kissing her arm along its trail. Stopping at her neck. Kissing it…he loved the way she was so ticklish there. As hard as she'd tried to fight it, she couldn't. And the fight…it had always led to more. A little shove back onto the bed, some pillow play, clothes flying everywhere… But these were dangerous thoughts, as he began to experience the stirrings of feelings and emotions he hadn't had in a long, long time. And while they were sexual, they weren't purely sexual the way they had been before. "It's dengue fever. Two members of one household."

"Hemorrhagic?"

Arlo raised his eyebrows in bold appreciation. "I see you know your dengue fever."

"A little. I did some reading on the plane. Not enough, but as much as I could to give me a good start here."

"Well, then—no. It's not hemorrhagic. But it did come on in the typlcal symptoms: high fever, headache, vomiting, muscle and joint pain, and a characteristic skin rash. We're at the end of it, too. This will probably be my last trip out there, which means the house calls on this one will be yours in the future, because dengue can relapse. So rather than having me do a daily check, you can do one every three or four days for a couple of weeks."

"Your treatment choice?" she asked.

"Supportive, for the most part. It's a mother and her five-year-old daughter. The rest of the family is fine."

"And by supportive you mean force liquids and treat other symptoms as they occur?"

"Exactly. Since it's a virus, that's about all we can do. Kanika and her daughter Achara went home from the hospital yesterday morning. They'd been here the week prior, and now Kanika's mother will be taking care of them until they're fully recovered. People here really opt for short-term stays. Or home care, when they can. So, from here on out it's mostly just rest and proper nutrition. And better mosquito netting."

"Do you see much dengue out here?" Layla asked.

"A fair amount, but not epidemic-sized. There have been efforts by the government to control the mosquitoes, but some of the remote areas such as this don't get a lot of help. I've petitioned for more netting and was allocated some, but not enough."

"Then I'll get some. How many do I need and who do I contact to make arrangements?"

"I've already petitioned for it, Layla. It will get here in due course."

"Could I get it here faster?"

"In the jungle, patience is a virtue. We get what we need, but sometimes we have to wait."

"And in the meantime people are being exposed to mosquito-borne disease. Why would you want to be patient about that?"

This was the same old Layla. Impatient for results. Impatient to move up. Impatient to get to the next thing on her list. He'd gotten used to it but coming from a place where impatience produced ulcers more than it did results, he'd never been one to indulge. And he worried that she did as it increased the chance that she would continually be dissatisfied in her life.

Impatient people risked feeling overwhelmed. They set themselves up for failure and got down on themselves when it happened. And they burned out easily. Layla was too bright to burn out, but her impatience was leading her straight down that path. He'd warned her over and over when they'd been together. She hadn't listened. Or maybe she'd thought she was somehow impervious to the pitfalls.

He didn't know which, but the Layla standing here with him right now hadn't budged from the Layla of the past. "Because that's the way it is here. We get what we need when it's available and always keep in mind there are twenty-five regions here, and each one has several hospitals just like ours, all needing the same things we need. Everybody gets served, but we have to realize that we're not the only ones in line."

"But what if I can cut that line?"

"I can't stop you. I never could. But be careful that cutting that line doesn't cost you somewhere later in your career. We're not impatient people out here, Layla. And we don't see the stress-related disease brought on by impatience here the way so many doctors see it in the more *civilized* societies. But you already know that."

"So what you're saying is you wouldn't support me trying to use my connections to get you what you need?"

"What I'm saying is we all do what we have to do. If buying netting from a private source is what you must do, then do it."

"And in return I'll get to listen to you complain."

"No. I don't complain about anything anyone donates, Layla. In fact, I'm grateful for it. And if you buy netting, I'll be grateful for that. But you do need to know what you're facing since you'll be working here for a while. It's rewarding and frustrating, in that order. And if you let it, it will tear you up."

"I don't know how you do it, Arlo."

He smiled. "Sometimes I wonder about that myself. But, for the most part, it works out. And I've got five hundred people living in the village and the same number living just outside who support me and help any way they can. And they're not impatient when they have to wait. I'm also not treating one ulcer in my whole practice."

"Point taken. But I still want to support you with some netting."

Ah, yes. The stubborn Layla got the last word. He'd expected it. And back when they'd been together, the making up that had come afterward had almost been worth the disagreement. It had always been more—intense. Arlo smiled, remembering. Almost missing those times. "And let me thank you in advance, because mosquitoes are a huge problem. So, tell me. Does your impatience get in the way of your medical practice? And I'm not trying to start something here. More like curious about an aspect of you I've always known."

"It's part of who I am as a doctor. When I order a test, I don't want to wait days for the results. When I order medications, I want them immediately. My patients expect that from me. So does your grandfather."

"He doesn't mind your impatience?"

"It gets results, so why should he?"

"You're always about the climb, aren't you?"

"That shouldn't come as news. And maybe time has escalated my impatience," she said, smiling. "However it works, it serves my patients well, and that's always the bottom line for me."

"But what about your own personal bottom line, Layla? I know you have an agenda, as most people do, but what happens to you if something derails it? What if you don't get this promotion? You've been working for it the whole time you've been a doctor, so what do you do with yourself when it doesn't happen? Do you take stock of the things you've put aside to get it? Do you regret what you've missed on that climb?"

"I don't know," she said. "For me, my life is designed around forward momentum. If that stopped, if I couldn't get where I wanted to go, I have no idea what I'd do. Maybe try someplace else. Maybe still keep pushing despite the roadblock."

"At what cost, though?"

"Do you really care, Arlo?"

"Surprisingly, yes. I know how you struggle to get ahead. I lived with it until I realized I couldn't compete with it."

"I'm sorry that happened," she said.

"I don't regret what we were, Layla. I walked away from us as a better man. But I did worry about your direction. In a lot of ways, it was much more difficult than mine. It still is." And, yes, he still worried. More than he should.

CHAPTER FOUR

THIS WAS CERTAINLY not what she'd expected, but she did like the more mature Arlo, with his dry wit and lack of sophistication. It was easy to see what she'd seen in him first time around, because most of it was still there, but better. Likability had never been a problem. But fundamental differences made up for that. No matter what else, he was a good man. Charitable. Kind. Nearly perfect in more ways than she remembered.

"You drive," Layla said, tossing her SUV keys to Arlo. It was sitting out front of the hospital, all washed and sparkly, thanks to the kindness of several villagers who'd pulled it out of the ditch and brought it to the hospital for her. Then detailed it. "Since you know where you're going and I don't."

They were on their way to visit Kanika, the woman who had had dengue fever.

"You're lucky as most of the way there is

on a real road. Dirt. A little rutted. But a road nonetheless."

"And by most of the way you're implying that some of the way is not?"

"I might be," he said, walking around the SUV, looking at every aspect of it. "Nice vehicle."

"A gift from my parents. Rather than telling me they were proud of me, they bought me a car. When I'm gone, you can have it to get you back and forth to those supplies you need and don't always have proper transportation to go and get. And, no, that's not the spoiled little rich girl doing this. It's the practical doctor who wants to help you."

"And the practical doctor in me appreciates your generosity."

"There was a time when you'd have said something cutting about me being a material girl."

"And there was a time when you were. But I was wrong to throw that back at you so much, especially at the end. I knew who you were, Layla, when we got together. You never made any pretense that you weren't. But we were extremely different people going in and our goals couldn't have been more different. We knew that, though, and most of the time we got around it. But when it was time to break up, I needed something to push me in that direction because I was really torn about doing what I'd set out to do or staying with you. So that's what I latched onto. I shouldn't have, and I'm sorry I did."

"You thought about staying?"

"All the time."

"But I drove you away. Isn't that why you left?"

He shook his head. "I always knew what I had to do. In the end, my sense of duty brought me home. You were always upwardly mobile. I was always homeward bound."

She knew that. She'd always known that and while he'd respected her direction, she hadn't respected his. "I wanted someone to love me more than they did their trappings. My parents never did. And you—I expected too much. In retrospect, we probably shouldn't have gotten involved the way we did."

"You regret it?" he asked.

She laughed. "Not a moment of it."

He hopped into the SUV and tossed his medical rucksack into the back seat. Layla did the same, and for the first several minutes of the ride they said nothing. Probably because they were both trying to process what had already been said. At least, that's what Layla was doing. But when Arlo stopped abruptly on the road, jumped out of the SUV and ran across to an old woman hobbling her way just off to the side, Layla called out the window, “Do you need me?”

“No. Waan has severe arthritis and I’m just offering her a ride home. She walks into the village once or twice a week to buy goods from the vendors, but she’s really not up to it.”

Layla watched him take the woman’s packages, then help her over to the SUV. Arlo was such a good man. If she’d thought that once since she’d known him, she’d thought that a million times. He cast her a boyish smile as he helped Waan into the back seat then took his place in the driver’s seat, next to Layla. Just looking at him and seeing the pleasure on his face in all the helpful things he did, she thought her heart would melt.

Did he know how drop-dead gorgeous he was? A little unkempt, but it worked for him. Always had. And maybe that was the expectation to beat all expectations. The perfect man for her, if there was such a thing, was more like Arlo, and less like any other man she’d ever met. Or might ever meet. “Is she on any kind of NSAID?” Layla asked, smiling back at the woman, who clearly only had eyes for Arlo.

“I’ve tried a few, but they bother her stomach. And the better-class drugs, like biological modifiers, aren't practical out here. Too much to monitor, too many lab tests."

"So, what does she take?"

"Nothing," Arlo said, turning off the main road onto a road that was little more than a path. "She decided she didn't want to worry about the side effects of pretty much anything I could prescribe, and as long as she can get around she's happy. Normally, one of her children will bring her to the village in a truck, but Waan is a proud, independent woman who likes to do it by herself when she can. Kind of like someone else I know."

"Have you researched any of the new drugs on the market? Maybe there's something..."

He shook his head. "She made her decision a couple of years ago, and I respect that. Medicine can cure many things, but for Waan it can't cure the indignities of always being needy. So she isn't." He stopped in front of a pleasant whitewashed cottage, and helped Waan out of the back seat. Then grabbed her packages and extended an arm to help her as they walked together, very slowly, up the path to the door. Once there, he handed her back her packages, bowed in respect to her, then hurried back to the SUV. "She's very traditional," he said. "Won't invite a man into her home unless there's a chaperone."

"Since she doesn't take any medicine, wouldn't she benefit from living in the village rather than isolated, so far outside it?"

"It's her home. She's lived every day of her almost eighty years there. And it was the home of her parents, her grandparents and possibly another generation before that. We might think living in the village would be better for her, but she thinks otherwise, and part of the medicine we practice out here is all tied up with respecting our patients for who they are and how they live, even when we think there might be a better alternative.

"Oh, and she said to tell you that you're welcome any time for tea. She likes having a lady doctor in the hospital." He chuckled. "Which may be code for her allowing you to do a physical on her. She won't let me even approach the subject."

"Maybe I can find a relatively safe histamine blocker or proton-pump inhibitor to take with an every-other-day NSAID. Or even something that combines ibuprofen with famotidine. A dose every other day would certainly be better than nothing. Do you think I could get something like that ordered?"

"You're really up on your pharmacopoeia. I'm impressed."

"I've had to treat too many gastric ulcers surgically, so to prevent the condition I have to be."

"Then I'll see what I can do about getting a trial sample in for Waan. Again, I'm impressed, Layla. I've thought of you in a lot of ways over the years, but never as a practicing surgeon, even though I knew you were one."

She laughed. "I do have my good moments." And one had just happened. This was the first time Arlo had ever complimented on her medical skills in any substantial way. In fact, it was the first time she'd ever had the feeling that he respected her abilities. That meant a lot, as his respect was something she'd always wanted more than almost anything else. And had never felt like she'd achieved.

Settling back into the seat, she closed her eyes, wanting to bask in the moment a little longer, but her basking was short-lived as Arlo swerved to avoid a rut that would have swallowed up a water buffalo, causing the seat belt to lock down on her. So she removed it to reset it and put it back on but, in that instant, when she wasn't belted in, he hit a bump that literally did send her sprawling almost into his lap. He immediately slowed the vehicle, and by the time she'd righted herself they were face to face, gazing into each other's eyes, only inches apart.

"Well, this feels awkward," he teased, stopping the vehicle while she maneuvered back into her seat. "Being close enough that we could have—"

"Kissed," she supplied.

"For starters."

"Maybe once," she said, fastening her belt. "But something tells me a kiss of convenience isn't nearly as good as one of passion. And a bump in the road doesn't really translate into passion."

"You sound more like I did all those years ago. Always overanalyzing everything and drawing conclusions rather than going with the moment."

"Live and learn," she said. "And I had a very good teacher." She'd also graduated at the top of her masterclass when it came to knowing how to protect her heart. And, as she was discovering, being near Arlo again made that very difficult. "Also, you may have known where you were going back then," she said, double-checking her safety strap, "but I'm not so sure about now, on this road, which is where your undivided attention should be."

He chuckled. "To think this is one of our better roads."

"No wonder your back aches. I'll bet it has as much to do with the bumps as it does falling through the roof."

"Actually, the road bothers my neck when I'm on the scooter."

"You need a hot tub, like I mentioned before."

"Actually, I'd settle for hot water in a real shower."

"Do you ever get away from here, Arlo? Not to go visit your family, but a day or two away, where you can kick back and do something nice for yourself?"

"Wish I could. But I can't afford it. I do go to a regional hospital a couple hours away from time to time, indulge in a hot shower, surf the internet, spend the night in a comfortable bed if my patient load here permits it. And then, only if the hospital has coverage."

"Well, it's not as nice as a luxury hotel, but I'm glad you have that."

He looked over at her. "You've changed, Layla. You're more accepting of things outside your norm."

She'd changed because she'd believed that if she could have been more for him, things might have ended up differently. So she'd worked on herself, trying hard to cultivate a broader vision. And a more tolerant one. "You grow up in the job. To be a good doctor, you have to. At least, I had to."

Arlo's recognition of her changes was nice. Very nice.

* * *

"Heads up," Arlo said, as they made their way up to the front door.

"What?"

"Heads up." He pointed to the snake, in all its green and black checkered glory, in the tree just in front of her, hanging down from a branch. "The element of surprise isn't really a good thing when it drops out of a tree onto your head." He stopped and waited until she caught up, then laid his hand across her back in a protective manner to escort her around the spot where the tree snake was plotting its move.

"It's a golden tree snake, and the bad thing is they conceal themselves pretty well in the trees. Another bad thing is they're very agile, and they bite quickly. Hurts like hell since they usually get you on the neck, face or shoulder. The good thing is they're only mildly venomous—usually just cause a little site reaction—and we do have the antivenin in stock if it turns out you're allergic.

"And just so you'll know, that's the snake you're most likely to find out here. Trees, walls, bushes. Meaning practice keeping your eyes on the ground while looking up at the same time because this little guy does like to have his way with you."

Once she was past the snake, Arlo reached

up and pulled him from his branch then carried him off into the bushes to let him go.

"You're even kind to the snakes," she said, as the trail narrowed to a barely passable width, and she was so busy looking for snakes she tripped over a tree root and, for the second time in less than half an hour, almost ended up in his arms. But this time she caught herself before she made the full fall, then jumped back when he attempted to grab hold of her to prevent her from hitting the ground. She slapped him, then laughed. "Thought you were another tree snake."

"Likely story," he said, stepping around her then taking her hand to pull her along. "And I try to be kind. What's the point in anything else?"

How could he just keep saying the right things over and over? How could she protect her heart from that? "So, you really know your herpetology," she said, deliberately avoiding anything that would pull her another step closer emotionally.

"Not as much as I should. Since I've lived here most of my life, you'd think I would have a background. But my up-close-and-personal relationship with snakes starts with me getting bitten and, so far, ending with me surviving. I can usually identify friend or foe, though."

"Sounds like I'll have to rely on you to take care of me. At least as far as the snakes go."

And he would. He had when they'd been together, when she'd been a wide-eyed innocent taking her first real trip into the world, and nothing had changed. She counted on that more than she'd ever wanted to.

"I always tried to, Layla. Even when you didn't want me to."

"I know, and I appreciated it, although I might never have told you." She brushed her hand over his cheek. "I've never *not* trusted you, Arlo. My problem was having that much trust in anyone scared me. Because having that kind of trust can lead to so much pain when it ends."

"How so?"

"Everybody has a personal motive. Brad, my failure of a fiancé, liked having me as a showpiece. Ollie's motive for my promotion brings notice to his surgery since female surgeons comprise less than twenty percent of all surgeons overall, and promoting one to a high position gives his surgery a lot of publicity. Even my own parents, for the sake of their careers, like to present a picture of a perfect family, which we're not."

"And me?"

"You simply came to me first as a friend then as a lover. And there was no pretext or motive to that. So, because of you, I learned to truly trust for the first time. Maybe the only time."

"I don't even know how to respond to that."

"Then don't. Take it for what it is. A simple truth. Something I've learned lately is that not everything needs a response. Some things can stand on their own." She smiled. "But thank you for giving me something to trust the way no one ever had before us, or even after us."

He studied her for a moment. Then finally said, "I think there were a lot of things we should have known about each other before, but didn't."

"Because we jumped in before we were ready. If we'd stood back and really looked at it, I don't think we would have leaped the way we did."

"Common sense isn't part of falling in love. We had the physical momentum and the friendship. But I think we lacked the common sense. At least I did. Otherwise I wouldn't have fallen so hard."

"But did you fall for me or the idea of what we should be?"

"Both. Not sure in what proportions, though. So…" He pointed to the two faces visible in the doorway. "I think we're being watched. Maybe because they're expecting a sweet."

Before he could pull a handful from his own

pocket, Layla reached into her pocket and beat him to it.

He chuckled. "You always were a quick learner."

"And you always were a good teacher."

By the time they'd approached the door, the children had already run out to join them, expecting the candy from Arlo but glad to take it from Layla.

"Friends for life," he said as they stood in the doorway.

"If only it was always that easy."

"Kanika, it's Doc Arlo. May I come in?"

The woman inside poked her head out the door to make sure, then stepped aside to let him in. Arlo spoke to her in Thai as she led them both back to a tiny, curtained-off area where a child lay on a mat on the floor. A beautiful child, with big brown eyes and thick black hair. And a big smile meant for Arlo. "Candy?" she asked in English.

This time he pulled another piece from his pocket and handed it to the girl, who stuffed it into her mouth as quickly as she could. "Achara is still feeling tired," he said to Layla. "She's not eating as well as her mother would like to see. Not drinking as much as she should either. Would you like to examine her while I take care of Kanika?"

"Love to," Layla said, then bent down to the child. "Hello, Achara," she said to the girl. "My name is Layla."

"Doc Layla," Arlo corrected. "The people out here respect the title 'Doc,' so it's always good to let them know you are a doc."

"My name is *Doc* Layla," Layla corrected. "And, while I know you don't understand my words, I promise I won't do anything that will hurt." She looked behind her as Arlo left the room, following Kanika to another part of the hut. "First, I want to do some general vital signs."

Temperature—elevated. Blood pressure—low. Pulse and respirations normal. No bad belly sounds. Lungs clear. But Achara did seem a little listless and, Layla noticed, she was struggling to stay awake. She also had a skin rash on her belly, back and arms.

"Do you hurt anywhere?" she asked the girl, even though Achara didn't understand. "Your tummy?" Layla pointed to Achara's tummy and made a scowling face, hoping the girl would understand her attempt at sign language.

Achara shook her head to indicate no. So Layla did the same things with several of her major joints—arms, hips, knees. Again, Achara shook her head. But when Layla addressed Achara's head, the girl nodded a yes and tears sprang to her eyes. Which meant she had a severe headache. So Layla looked into her eyes then in her nose, only to find signs that the little girl was experiencing nosebleeds.

"Arlo," Layla called out. "I need a second opinion, if you don't mind."

"Right here," he said, entering the curtained-off space. "What's the matter?"

"She has a mild version of the symptoms you'd see in hemorrhagic dengue. What I want is for you to double-check for me, since this is way out of my field of expertise."

"Out here, there will be many times when you don't have someone to double check. I'll do it this time because you haven't even been here very long, but in the future, go with your gut. If you think she's gone hemorrhagic, then proceed accordingly. You're a good doctor. Trust yourself." He pulled his stethoscope from his cargo pants pockets and listened to Achara's chest and belly. Then felt her forehead. Looked at her eyes…

"She's complaining of a headache," Layla said.

Arlo nodded, and kept on with his appraisal by looking up the girl's nose. Then he pressed her belly again and took another listen. "Good catch," he finally said. "But getting Kanika to allow me to take her back to the hospital isn't going to be easy. I was worried about the girl when she took her home but, short of physically forcing her to stay, there was nothing I could do."

"Maybe if you emphasize now that her daughter's in danger, that her condition has gotten worse?"

"Kanika already knows all that. In fact, she told me that Achara wasn't doing as well as she was just a couple of days ago."

"And she still won't let you take her to the hospital?"

Arlo shook his head. "People die there. The villagers know that, and I think it scares Kanika, leaving her daughter alone there. Achara was only there the first time because Kanika was there as well."

"Does she have a husband who might grant us permission?"

"He died in an accident several years ago."

Layla let out a frustrated sigh. "Can we allow Kanika to stay with her daughter? Maybe assume some of her nursing care?"

"We can. If she'll agree to it."

"She'll agree to it, Arlo. She's a mother and her child comes first."

"Since when did you get so...motherly? We never even talked about having children because I believed you'd choose career over having them."

"And I would have. Still would. But that doesn't mean I can't have a few maternal instincts floating around. You know, some maternal instinct. Maybe not for being a mother myself so much but for mothers in general. A good mother will always protect her child. Like yours did."

He thought, for a moment, about the way his mother had protected him, and sacrificed for him, and he could see Layla doing the same. Even though they'd never talked about having a child, he'd known she'd have been a very good mother by the little ways she'd taken care of him. Providing a nice home even when she wasn't domestic, allowing him space when he needed it without asking why, being there when he'd needed her and wouldn't ask. Nursing him through bouts of flu or common colds. "You're always full of surprises, Layla."

"Or maybe you just never noticed the things in me that were always there."

At the time he hadn't and now he was sorry for that. "It was my loss," he said.

"Our loss, Arlo. It was our loss."

As it turned out, Layla's suggestion worked quite well. Kanika was more than happy to work at the hospital, and while she was there she extended her care to a couple of other patients. Basic care. Nothing along the line of anything medical. But delivering meals, changing bed sheets, pouring drinks of water. It was a tremendous help, and he was pleased that Layla had suggested it.

It showed him a different side of her—the side where she took the smaller aspects of patient care into consideration. When he'd thought she was all about the bigger picture, he'd been wrong. She was much more insightful and well-rounded than he'd known.

And now, on the third day of Kanika's duties, she was rearranging the furniture to make it more convenient, recruiting new volunteers to come in and cook, and was in the process of making curtains for bare windows, courtesy of several women who donated fabric…an odd assortment of colors and textures. All this due largely to Layla's simple suggestion. It was all good.

And Layla, with Samron's assistance, was working just as hard, going on the afternoon house calls for him, taking the older woman with her to translate, while he stayed back and kept the hospital open. She also took morning calls at the clinic while he was out in the field. Or sleeping.

Even more good coming about because of something he'd never seen in Layla. Or something he'd totally overlooked. While he'd always known she was a hard worker, he'd always thought of her as someone who didn't join in. But that's all she was doing here. Joining in wherever she could. And seeming to enjoy it.

Sadly, they didn't ever stop to chat, unless it had something to do with a patient, and they didn't even take a meal together. It seemed like the only time they really crossed paths was at night, when they were both getting ready for bed. He could see Layla in silhouette through the curtain as she readied herself for sleep. The first night he'd averted his eyes for the sake of being polite.

But his memories of her perfection, of her beauty, of the pleasures her naked body had given him had taken hold, and those memories were more vivid than anything he could see through the curtain. And more intrusive, penetrating every pore in his body. Trying to work their way into more places than he wanted. She was so beautiful, and curvy, and she had a graceful purpose in every movement.

After that first night of trying not to look, and trying not to remember, he couldn't help but watch the shadowed image of her, the elegant movements, the way she went about things in the same order each night. Layla was all he'd ever wanted in a woman, which had made his only real attempt at relationships after they'd split up impossible. Nobody compared. And it wasn't just in the physical sense. But in her intellect, even her ambition.

Layla was a perfect package and even as he'd walked away from her all those years ago, he'd known he would never find that kind of perfection or determination in anyone else. That had been true then, and still was now. He was a spoiled man—spoiled for something he could not hold onto. Which, little by little, was forcing him to come to terms with the way the rest of his life would be lived.

What would it have been like if he'd chosen another path—one with Layla at the end of it, waiting there for him with open arms?

CHAPTER FIVE

STANDING IN THE doorway of his hut, looking out, Arlo watched the rain for a few minutes. It wasn't the rainy season yet, but it was getting close. Layla was asleep, but his memories and thoughts made him too restless to sleep. And the rain beating down so heavily on the roof, sounding like gunfire, didn't help either.

There was too much of the past swirling around in his head. There were so many good things he'd overlooked or ignored. And now the heavy impact of having her here was something he'd never expected. She was igniting things in him that had died out all those years ago. Giving him hopes to latch onto again, even though he knew he shouldn't. Layla had always made him happy. But he had to be cautious because this was only temporary, just like last time had been.

Without looking back at the curtain, or the now dim image on the other side, Arlo launched into the downpour and bounded across the road to the hospital so quickly it barely raised a blip in his consciousness. Why was he there? He wasn't even sure about that. Probably to occupy space where Layla wasn't distracting him. Where his whole life wasn't distracting him. Where he wasn't questioning his choices and promises.

"Promises," he said aloud. The one he'd made to his mother to look after his dad after she was gone. The one he'd made his dad to take his mother's place as a doctor after she was gone. The first hadn't worked out since his dad had left shortly after the funeral. Which had left Arlo stuck here in a practice meant for two but now as the only doctor.

And in the early days, when he'd thought about going back to civilization, to Layla, something had always stopped him. A fever outbreak. A critically injured patient who would have died without his help. People who depended on him. People who trusted him to take care of them. That was a lot of responsibility to carry around.

But to toss it aside would be to walk away from someplace where he was needed. And maybe there was a little arrogance mixed in with that—the kind that told him he was the only one who could do this job. That was all about *his* need, though. The need to be needed. Layla had always wanted him, but she'd never needed him. And the distance between those was wider than the universe.

Still, in his more thoughtful moments, when ego wasn't taking over, and the hurt of not being needed by the woman he'd needed went away, he simply saw the need of the village as the binding element. If he left, no one would come to replace him. Like no one had replaced Layla.

Arlo knew these were crazy, mixed-up emotions, but they were all he had. He'd offered Layla his world, she'd turned it down. In retrospect it had been selfish as he'd never stopped to realize how important her world was to her. And had she offered it to him, he would have turned it down, probably with some lame excuse that it wasn't altruistic enough. But in the end, to give yourself over to caring for the sick was altruistic no matter where it happened. That was one of the last things his mother had told him but, by then, it had been too late. Layla had moved on without him. How did he know? In a word—Ollie. Then another three words from Ollie—*"Bad mistake, Arlo."* Then another six—*"How could anyone be so blind?"*

The glum periods didn't get him down too often, though. Not anymore. He hated the feeling, the despair that occasionally took over, because that wasn't him. Couldn't be him, if he wanted to keep doing what he was doing. Which he did. But right now he wasn't on his game. And the last time he'd felt that way had been the evening he'd made the decision that he had to leave her. His mother had been sick, he'd had to go home, he'd asked her to go with him, and she'd refused.

Such a bad time in his life, which had got even worse later when he'd realized how badly he'd wandered through it. But at the time all he could see was that loving Layla wasn't enough for her. She'd needed the one thing he'd never be able to give her—an outlet for her ambition. Anyway, all that was water under the bridge now. He'd made his choices based on the only life he'd known, and she'd made hers based on the very same thing. So, maybe they hadn't been in love the way it's truly defined, but there were too many things yet to explore. So the ending had been left hanging. Not resolved. Simply let go of.

Did he love her? That was the one question he'd never explored too deeply because there was no answer to it. In many ways he had. But in all the ways necessary to make her happy? Obviously not. It was more obvious now than before. But what good did knowledge do when he still had no answers? Well, at least he had his work, and that was a good thing because he loved it here. That was the one thing he didn't doubt, when pretty much everything else right now was shrouded in confusion.

Arlo tiptoed into the ward to look at Achara. She was sleeping peacefully, the way a child should. And Kanika was curled up in the bed next to her.

He looked across the aisle at another patient who'd simply wandered in to sleep. It happened. People simply came when they wanted something and for Niran Metharom, who was sleeping face down on a cot in the corner, it was when he was feeling the effects of having had too much to drink.

Kosum Bunnag, an octogenarian with gastric complaints, came because of gastric upset. Her problem was eating mangos, which didn't agree with her. She knew it and suffered the consequences of gorging herself on her favorite food, and expected Arlo to make it better. If he wasn't there, she simply took a bed and waited. Or slept. Tonight she was sleeping in the corner opposite Niran.

And while nobody here was really sick except Achara, this was his world. It's where he knew himself. Besides, where else would people just admit themselves to a hospital and not even bother to find the doctor?

After taking a quick look at all three of his patients, satisfied they were doing well, Arlo tucked himself into his exam room, ready to peruse a pile of outdated medical journals as sleep simply wasn't in him. But thoughts of Layla were.

"Was there an emergency or something?" she asked him, coming into the exam room, dripping wet from the rain, about fifteen minutes after he'd made himself comfortable.

He looked up, surprised to find her there. Soaked to the bone, with a lab jacket they kept in the hospital more for impression than use pulled over her T-shirt and cargo shorts. She looked so damned adorable he caught himself in a familiar ache. "What?"

"I heard you leave a few minutes ago, and I wondered if you needed help with anything."

"Nope. It's just a restless night. I have them every so often and use the time to catch up on some journal reading. And it's a good thing I did because a couple of people admitted themselves."

"Anything serious?"

He shook his head. "They're fine. Mostly looking for a dry bed and a little reassurance, I think. When they wake up, I'll give them each another a look before I send them on their way."

"So, in the meantime, you read journals."

"Got to keep up some way."

"How do you get them since there's no mail delivery?"

"I print them out at the elephant rescue when I'm there. They have a computer with satellite internet, and a very iffy connection for mobile phones. It's a trade-off. I get to use their conveniences when I need to, in exchange for my half-day at the elephant wash. And that rover I have access to when I need a vehicle."

"Elephant rescue?"

A smile crept to his lips. "I meant to tell you about that. Guess it slipped my mind."

"Tell me what?"

"We donate time at the elephant rescue. We trade our services for the use of the various things they have that we don't."

"And by donate you mean…"

"Whatever's required. Usually we work with the babies. You know, play with them, wash them—simple things."

"A baby elephant wash?"

"Just part of a day, once a week. It works out."

"I'm assuming I'll be expected to—?"

"It's strictly voluntary," Arlo said. "But if you can sleep with a civet cat, I'm pretty sure you can relate to a baby elephant."

"As long as I don't have to sleep with it, too."

Arlo chuckled. "Not usually."

"Then life is good." Layla entered the exam

room and hopped up on the exam table, since her only other sitting option was the floor, which was where Arlo was sitting. Cross-legged, barefoot, with his back braced by the wall. "Especially if I can get good phone reception there. Or can log onto my social media page."

"What you learn really fast is that you don't necessarily need the modern conveniences here. Since I grew up here, I didn't have them at my disposal, and I learned how to live life just fine without them. Although I do admit I enjoy surfing the internet every now and then. Or playing an online game."

"Your parents traveled, though, didn't they?"

"Most of the time, yes. A month here, a month there. There are a lot of villages in the area, so they didn't keep a home base the way I do. It was a fun way to grow up, though. Of course, it was all I knew."

"But when you ventured into the outside world..."

"It was a culture shock to some extent. But my parents prepared me for that. So, other than not fitting in too well, it was OK. And my less than sophisticated ways did attract your attention."

"You sat on the floor, cross-legged, when we were attending lectures. There were perfectly good desks but you always chose the floor." She laughed. "And remember that day I caught you staring at the wall? It was like you'd never seen a wall before."

"Hadn't seen that many of them. And I liked the composition of it. It was…sturdy. In the huts where we generally stayed, walls were flimsy, for the most part."

"But it was a wall."

"And it brought me to your attention, didn't it?"

"Speaking of bringing something to your attention, did you see that the shipment of mosquito netting came in? I didn't even know it had been ordered."

He wiggled his phone at her. "After you offered, I went down the road a bit, placed the order—it's in your name, by the way. The bill will be forthcoming."

"So, who delivered it?"

"A friend from the regional hospital. I had it sent there and he dropped it by. He's the nurse who comes out to help when we're desperate. And, yes, he signed for a shipment of drugs and brought them along as well. Paid for courtesy of the government's health program."

"Do you ever get desperate having to rely on so many people?"

"Sometimes. But then I get over it because

there are a lot of more serious things to worry about."

"I don't suppose I ever realized how resilient you were. I always knew you were a brilliant surgeon, but I think I tried not to picture this part of you."

"Why?"

"Because I knew it would eventually come between us." She pulled her wet T-shirt away from her skin. "Mind if I put on a dry hospital gown?"

Too bad…he was enjoying the wet look. Enjoyed her with the dry look as well. In fact, there was never a look he didn't like when it came to Layla. And he'd probably seen all of them. "Help yourself."

She returned to the exam room in a thin gown that was a dozen sizes too large for her frame, but this time she sat down on the floor next to him rather than on the table, then cuddled up to him. Something that came so naturally she didn't even realize she was doing it. But he did. Back then, now. And his natural response would have been to put his arms around her and snuggle in even more, which he wasn't going to do.

"I used to enjoy this," she said, leaning her head on his shoulder. "Curling up in front of the fireplace together, even if all we were doing was studying. Too bad we never had much time for it."

"We didn't have much time for anything together, Layla. Too much work, too much study."

She laughed. "The life of a doctor. Coming from a long line of them, I'm sure you knew what to expect. But I didn't. All I saw was the glamorous side—from television and movies. Even from when I fell out of a tree and broke my leg when I was eight and spent a couple of weeks in the hospital, being attended to by the most gorgeous doctor I'd ever seen. At least, gorgeous in the eyes of a child who was totally in love with the image of him, especially the way people looked at him—with so much respect.

"That's why I became a doctor, you know. I always remembered how people looked at him and that's how I wanted them to look at me. Probably also to impress him since I decided, at the tender age of eight, I was going to marry him, despite the fact he was probably forty." She laughed. "Only in the mind of a child, right?"

"A child who set her course when she was eight and never left it. So, would you go back and do it again?" he asked, taking care not to touch her in any way, since he knew their history and remembered what a single touch could start. Not that he was a man who wouldn't want that. But with Layla there were painful aftershocks. Those were what he wanted to avoid as he'd suffered them the first time and had come out unscathed. Well, relatively unscathed. She *had* made him a much more mindful person in that regard. "Medical school to surgeon. Knowing what you know now, would you still make that choice?"

"In a heartbeat. My childhood dream doctor became the basis for a lifelong passion and I never wavered in what I wanted after I was eight. So, what about you when you were eight?"

"When I was eight, I was already a medic of sorts. Fetching supplies my parents needed in the moment, making sure their medical bags were stocked properly. All except for the drugs, of course. Sometimes they'd let me treat minor things like scratches. You know, wash, antiseptic, bandage."

"And you never changed either."

"It's what I knew."

"No regrets you kept it up?"

"My only regret was that I didn't have the opportunity to work with them after I was a real doctor. I wanted that, worked hard to push myself through so I could have it, but it didn't happen."

"I'm sorry," she said, reaching over and taking his hand.

The muscle in his right forearm twitched under her touch, but he didn't pull himself away from her because he liked being where he was. Always had with Layla. "So am I. But what I have now…" He shrugged. "Almost all of it's good."

"Me, too," she said. "I never meant to work for Ollie, given the connection you and I had, but when he made me the offer…"

"He's a great judge of talent. To succeed in his world, you have to be." He smiled. "To my knowledge, he's never been wrong in the doctors he's chosen to work in his surgery. You included."

"I thought for a while it was his way of trying to get us back together."

"Nope. He's not the type to interfere. My guess is that he assumed you'd come back to Thailand with me and was thrilled when you didn't because he'd get his shot at you."

"Well, he's been good to me. And I love working where I do."

He didn't want to let go of her hand, didn't want to get up and walk away. But nothing was stirring at this late hour and they both needed to sleep. She in the relative comfort of the hut and he…someplace where she wasn't. "Look, we're in the rare position of no late-night calls to make and unless something comes in, as Homer said in his *Odyssey*, 'There is a time for many words, and there is also a time for sleep.' So, on that note, Homer and I bid you goodnight."

Unfortunately, what he intended as a dignified exit from the room turned into something much less. As he stood, his back gave out and stopped him halfway to his feet. "So much for the grand departure," he muttered. Then forced himself upright, inch by inch.

Layla laughed. "Off with the shirt, Arlo. This is ridiculous, especially when I can help you." To prove her point, she cracked her knuckles, then patted the exam table. "Face down, get comfortable."

"Don't do this, Layla," he moaned, knowing that so much of her touch would drive him insane.

"Doctor's orders, or I might have to declare you unfit for duty."

"I'm the boss here. Remember?"

"And I'm the one with the magic fingers. Remember?"

He moaned again. "I'll be fine."

"After I'm done with you." She pushed away from him, went to the supply cabinet, pulled out a bottle of jasmine oil, a gift from a patient, and returned to the exam table.

"I'm not going to smell like flowers," he protested.

"What? Not manly enough to be secure in wearing a delicate scent?" She rubbed some on her hands, then bent down and waved them at him. "Tempted?"

"Not yet," he said, enjoying the flirt. He used to enjoy their lighter moments, the teasing, the playfulness. It was one of the things he'd missed most after they'd broken up. "What else have you got?"

She pulled down the neck of his T-shirt just a little and rubbed some of the oil across his chest. "That?"

He chuckled. "How is it that you're the only woman I've ever known who could get away with making me smell like jasmine?"

"Just one of my many charms," she said, patting the exam table again. "So, like I said, shirt off..."

Naturally, he gave in. He always had, because his little pretenses of resistance had never gone very far with her. All she had to do was—

"Let me help you out of your shirt," she said, grabbing hold of the bottom of it and slowly lifting it over his stomach.

Yes, that was always the start of it.

Then her journey went to his chest and it was agonizingly slow. On purpose? Was she taking this so slowly to torture him? Or was he simply primed to be tortured by any intimacy from her? And this was so tactile, so intimate. The chills her fingers were causing attested to that.

"Are you able to get it over your head on your own, or do you need help?"

Another time, he would have taken the help, prolonged it, begged for more. But not now. So, rather than answering, he tugged his shirt over his head and lay on the exam table as quickly as possible, hoping that the thoughts in his head would turn clinical rather than stirring. "This isn't going to take long, is it?" he asked, trying to dispel the mood sliding down over him.

"As long as it needs to take," she said, taking her place at the side of the table then applying pressure to his lower back.

"In case you were wondering, it's my serratus posterior inferior. It lies…"

Layla laughed. "I showed up to class that day, Arlo. I know where it is." Lower back, and in his case the right side. Which was where she positioned her hands and began a light rub, which elicited an immediate moan. "You're lucky all you did was pull some muscles. Next time you're up on a roof look where you're stepping or you might injure something more important than your serratus posterior inferior."

"Ah, yes, lovely bedside manner. Lecture the patient who's in excruciating pain." He moaned again, and this time sucked in a sharp breath.

"Nice hands," he said on exhalation. "I think they've improved with age."

"What? You didn't like my massages back then?"

"Different kind of massages. Those were meant to lead to other things. This one is meant to cure me." It had been so long since he'd experienced a woman's touch in any meaningful way he'd almost forgotten what pure pleasure felt like. But this was it—Layla's touch. Always had been. And as far as he was concerned, this was a massage that could last for hours, or forever, and he wouldn't get tired of it.

"Sounds like the rain's letting up," she said, after he'd been dead silent, except for an occasional moan, for the past five minutes. She hadn't intended this massage to turn into a flirt, but something had grabbed hold of her, and she was fully involved in it long before she realized what she was doing. So many things just seemed to come naturally with Arlo, things she'd taken for granted when they'd been together. And now they were reminders of what she'd let go.

"Then maybe you should go back to the hut and try to get some sleep."

"Are you sure? Because I could keep doing this for a while longer."

"But I can't, Layla. It's—it's making me think things I shouldn't be thinking."

She understood that as she was probably thinking many of the same thoughts. Maybe she was trying to go too far based on something that was no longer there. Or simply getting caught up in the past. Whatever the case, Arlo was right. So she stepped back from the table and picked up a towel to wipe her hands. "Then you'll stay here?" Honestly, she hoped he would because she didn't want to face him for a while. Not until she'd better sorted out her intentions.

"I've got insulin rounds in a couple of hours, and I do want to check my patients here when they wake up, so yes. I'll stay here."

And that was all they said. Layla took the hint to leave and did. Trudged across the muddy road as fast as she could to get away from him, only to find Chauncy, who'd decided not to be a night prowler in the rain, curled up on her cot. "It was a huge mistake," she told the cat as she sat down beside him. "All mine." And one she wouldn't make again.

He'd already checked and released his two late-night admissions and made three house calls by the time Layla wandered into the hospital the next morning. "Sleep well?" he asked, hoping she didn't feel as awkward as he did. And drained because every time he'd tried shutting his eyes her image had been there. Followed by memories, and images of things in the past. Meaning he'd had no sleep whatsoever.

"Well enough. So, how's your back this morning?"

"Much better." That was true. Even just those few minutes under her fingertips had produced more relief than he'd expected. "I think you could have a future as a massage therapist, if that's what you wanted." The air between them was heavy with trepidation and watchfulness. There was no way to get around it other than avoid it. And the best avoidance was work, which he was anxious to get back to. "The patient list is on the desk," he said. "I didn't sleep well so I worked."

"Because of your back?"

He shook his head. "There were too many things rattling around in my brain."

"You used to do that. Get so caught up in your responsibilities you couldn't sleep. Wish I could do something to help. Maybe chamomile tea? Maybe I can order you some when we get to the elephant rescue?"

He nodded and smiled. What was wrong with him wouldn't be fixed by any kind of tea, but he appreciated her gesture. That was always one of Layla's best points—her tenderness. "I'm not used to having anybody take care of me anymore. At least, not the way you used to."

"Sometimes it was the only way we could find time together." She laughed. "You didn't know, but because you were always so busy going one way while I was going another, I actually created a list of things I could do for you—other than the obvious—that would slow you down and allow me some time with you."

He arched surprised eyebrows. "Seriously?"

She nodded. "You couldn't resist homemade chocolate cookies, but when you knew I was baking them, you'd hang around for as long as it took for the first batch to come out of the oven. Most of the time I was very slow getting that first batch done."

"I never knew."

"I had my ways."

"Please tell me that walking up the five flights of stairs to our apartment was for health reasons like you said, and not just a way to have a little more time together. Because you know how I hated those stairs."

"Almost as much as I enjoyed the view walking behind you."

"You little minx," he said, laughing out loud. "I never had a clue."

"You weren't meant to. But it was all fun and

games, Arlo. We always knew that's what it was between us. And now?"

"I work. And there's no one here to bake chocolate-chip cookies. Sometimes I wish there was."

"It's got to be a lonely life for you out here. I can't even begin to imagine how you get by."

"One day at a time. Or sometimes hour by hour."

Finally, they were back on track and she liked that. Liked the good things they'd been through together—moments like this one. Wished there'd been more back then. Even wished there could be more now. "After we were done, and after you got here, did you ever wish you'd chosen a different life? Or redesigned the one you had?"

"Not after I got back, but I did have this brief time after we split when I thought I didn't want to come back. A lot of that was tied to you. And Ollie. He'd paid my tuition, as you knew, and he pressured me for about a year to come in with him because he honestly didn't realize that I loved what I was doing here. When he figured it out, that's when he stopped."

"And when he came after me."

"Score one for Ollie. He's always had an eye for pretty girls and an instinct for getting the best doctors. With you, he got both."

"And you got?"

"Everything here. The village. The jungle. The people. Home is home, and this is mine. In the end, it's what I wanted more than anything else."

"Including me."

"Maybe the biggest regret of my life. But it was always a losing cause. This is where I was meant to be."

"Here. In this village. This is what cost me… you. I didn't like it, Arlo, but over time I accepted it. Oh, and how do you pronounce the village's name? Since I lost you to it I should, at least, know how to call it out by name."

He laughed then said something she would never come close to pronouncing. Not unless she was much further along in her Thai language skills, which wouldn't be happening in her two-month stay. "The meaning is village by the big fig tree."

"The tree you see just at the entrance to the village?"

He nodded. "It's a symbol of enlightenment, believed to bring good fortune."

"Well, if you're happy, it's brought you good fortune. So, let me grab that patient list and get started because—" Because almost having him was worse than not having him at all. And sometimes, even now, her heart just hurt.

"Because don't we have an afternoon appointment with the elephants?"

Arlo hid himself in the bushes near the elephant reserve and watched Layla playing with the baby assigned to her care. She looked so happy, playing and splashing. He hadn't often seen her abandon herself this way, and he truly wished she could find more joy in her life. But she went about her life so methodically, like she was laboring under the biggest weight in the world.

Emerging from the bushes after watching her for a while, Arlo waved at Layla as he passed near her, and found himself totally drawn into her smile as she waved back. He'd always enjoyed finding those things that caused her to smile like that or gave her an unexpected thrill or happiness she hadn't expected. She could be like a child on Christmas, excited to open all her presents. And he'd been lucky enough to be part of that occasionally. "Care for a mango?" he called across the compound. "Your baby might love them."

Layla turned to look at him, which was her first mistake. Her second was allowing the hose to point away from the baby. In that split second of distraction the baby grabbed the hose from her hand and started to run off with it, as any toddler, elephant, human or otherwise, might do. And in doing that the baby, named Tika, bumped into Layla, sending her sprawling into the big, orange plastic tub filled with muddy water where Tika had been playing. Seeing that as an opportunity to play, Tika slid into the tub with Layla, pinning Layla to the side at first, then trying to crawl onto her lap as she struggled to pull herself up.

"I see you have a situation," Arlo called out. It was too funny not to laugh, which he and everyone else did, as Layla struggled to get out from under the affectionate ministrations of the two-hundred-plus pounds of Tika, who thought this was the best playtime ever, and wasn't about to let her new playmate out of the water.

"Did I mention that baby elephants love to play?" he said, walking over to the edge of the tub, not to lend Layla a hand but to enjoy a more close-up view of playtime in the elephant compound.

Covered with muddy water, she simply looked up at him. No smile. No frown. No expression whatsoever on her face. "I think she's sprained my ankle," she said, her voice flat. "Could you help me out of here? I want you to have a look at it." With that, she extended her hand to Arlo, who was already feeling terrible about Layla's injury.

"Maybe it's just a twist," he said, as he took hold of her, which was his first mistake. His second was to lean slightly over the tub in case he had to lift her from the water. In that instant, what he never saw coming happened. Layla pulled him down into the tub with Tika and her.

"The twist, Doctor," she said, her face still as serious as it could be, "is that you fell for it." Then she smiled.

"What the—?" he sputtered, still trying to figure out what had just happened when Tika, who was thoroughly enjoying having two playmates now, slid herself over the top of Arlo then splashed around until half the water was out of the tub.

That was the opportunity Layla needed to hop out and grab the hose, then start to refill the tub with water, much to Tika's delight, as she now nuzzled Arlo like a kitten might nuzzle its mother. "I think she loves you," Layla said, turning the hose directly on Arlo. "In a muddy kind of way."

He sputtered as the water hit his face, which, to Tika, was an open invitation to slide across him again, but go on out the opposite side of the tub, leaving Arlo sitting in the middle of a pool of dirty water while Layla continued to hose him down, still trying to keep a straight face.

"You know this isn't funny," he said, attempting to stand—another invitation for Tika to rejoin him in the tub and knock him back into the water.

Layla finally laughed. Smiled, laughed again and wiped at the streams of muddy water dripping from her hair. "When it was me in there, you thought it was."

Arlo managed to slide away from Tika and get himself over to the edge of the tub. When he looked up at Layla, who was still laughing, and who also turned the water back on him, his heart skipped a beat. There was such a vulnerability about her when she let herself go. Not only was she stunningly beautiful underneath all that mud that was caking on her now, her laugh was infectious. It made him laugh along with her.

"When it was you in here, it *was* funny," he said, crawling on his knees then looking over his shoulder to make sure he wasn't going to fall victim to a playful Tika attack again. But she'd found his sack of mangos and was helping herself to a little treat, which gave Arlo a chance to get out of the tub. He held out his hand for the hose, but Layla refused. Instead she turned the water on him again. "You really don't think I'd fall for that old trick, do you?" she asked, taking a couple of steps back from the tub. "You'd have to be pretty naïve to—"

Before she could finish her sentence, Arlo lunged out of the water and grabbed the hose away from her, threatening to turn it on her now. "Mud suits you, so I really should just let you stay as you are," he said, laughing, as she came at him and tried to grab away the hose.

She made another jump at him but again failed to get the hose. "You know you're just asking for more trouble," she warned him.

"And *you* know I could pick you up and drop you right back in the tub for more Tika play," he said, turning the hose on her.

"If you can catch me." Layla made another lunge at him, this time with the intent of knocking him back into the tub, but he turned the water on her face, and by the time she wiped away enough to see, he'd ducked to the other side of the tub, still hanging onto the hose.

"Oh, I can catch you," she said, edging her way around the other side, hoping to trap him against the fence so she could grab the hose and claim victory.

But he was too fast for her. In fact, as she got so close to him all he could see was the outline of her breasts through her wet T-shirt, he knew he had to get away as the thoughts in his head were suddenly going places he didn't want them to go. So he intended to drop the hose and sprint off to his own baby, Lamon. But before the hose hit the ground, she grabbed it up and hit him with a spray of water as he, too, tried to get across the tub, his intention being to surrender his shirt to cover her up. "Um, Layla," he said, deliberately keeping his eyes above her shoulders, "I think you need to…" As he started to unbutton his shirt, she hopped into the tub with him, knocked him down, then stood over him, aiming the hose over his head with one hand and fist-pumping the air in victory with her other. "Victory is sweet," she said, stepping back and offering Arlo a hand to help him up.

"You really need to cover up," he said, almost in a whisper, struggling now to keep his eyes averted. Being polite wasn't so easy, though, when temptation was so close. "Before someone else sees you."

She looked down at herself, then laughed. "Why, Doctor, you're a bit of a prude, aren't you?" She did try to pluck the stretchy fabric away from her skin, but that was almost impossible.

"Not a prude so much as not wanting everybody here to get a look at you the way I'm seeing you. Especially since you're their doctor."

"Prude," she said, turning the hose on him again.

He was surprised by her lack of modesty, and he was enjoying not only the view but the spontaneity. Was this the real Layla? The one who came out of her shell when she wasn't taking herself so seriously? "Look, let me get up and give you my shirt, OK? And next time wear something more decent." Unfortunately, as she backed away to allow him to rise up to his knees, Tika decided it was time to play again and ran toward the tub. Hopped in. Knocked Arlo back down, as well as Layla, who landed on top of him.

"So, now what?" she asked, still holding onto the hose like it was a trophy.

He smiled, bracing himself for what he knew was about to happen. And it did. Layla turned the hose so the water sprayed down his head, and as he went to grab it out of her hand, she kissed him. It happened so quickly, so innocently, he wasn't even sure it had happened. But the look of total surprise on her face told him it had, and it had surprised her as much as it had him. He didn't react, though. Caution was the better choice here. Wait and see what she did next. All his hopes were pinned on another kiss, but Tika had something else in mind as she slid slightly to the side of him to start a new game, which was much the same as the old one. Water, mud and lots of attempts to sit on their laps.

Certainly, it was safe. But it was also disappointing. And, as he was dwelling on that, Tika lunged, flipping him over, which pinned Layla underneath him. For what seemed like an eternity, he simply stared down at her.

"Mud or not, you're a beautiful woman," he said, lowering his head to capture her lips. But after a brief kiss, which was more a prelude than a real kiss, the way they'd used to kiss, he moved to her eyelids, kissing first the left, then the right. Feeling the slippery mud between their bodies, realizing it heightened the moment rather than taking away from it. Then he kissed her lips again, this time harder, but the sensation ignited him so quickly, he pulled back much sooner than he'd intended.

Layla was surprised judging from the look on her face, possibly by the kiss, possibly by his restraint, and she groped for him, tried to pull him back, but the mud oozed through her fingers, causing her hands to slip away. Yet she reached up and touched his lips. Tickled them the way he remembered, running a single finger from corner to corner. Back and forth, over and over until he could no longer endure it.

Then, without thought, he was kissing her again, slipping his hand underneath her muddy, wet shirt, now transparent enough to see her nipples. And that's when he stopped himself. Pulled back, only farther this time, and simply stared down at her. She felt so good underneath him again. Too good. And, yes, the consequences could be devastating. They had been once, and that was something he never wanted to go through again.

Which was why he rolled off Layla, got himself out of the tub, then removed his shirt and handed it to her. “Put it on,” he said, sounding almost grumpy, even to *his* ears. Because, despite what he knew, he still did want to kiss her. And more.

CHAPTER SIX

"EXCUSE ME, DOCTORS," said a tiny old woman, keeping her distance from the very wet, very muddy Arlo and Layla.

She was Sylvie Fontaine, the director of the facility. A volunteer there herself once.

"We have a visitor in need of medical assistance."

Her voice was soft, her accent distinctly French, and the look on her face totally amused, probably because of what she'd just witnessed.

"He's complaining of an upset stomach."

Arlo and Layla looked at each other as Layla buttoned his shirt to be modest while he stood there, bare-chested, looking sexier than any man she'd ever seen in her life. His abs were tight, the proverbial six-pack. His chest bare and broad. His arms strong. Everything about Arlo exuded strength, and she was surprised by her reaction to him. He was beautiful, even if still muddy. Perfect. A man any woman would want.

A man she would want if that's why she was here. Which wasn't as that kind of thing, even briefly, was too much of a distraction and she had goals. "How long?" Layla asked, fighting hard to refocus on work.

"He wasn't feeling well last night, and he hasn't gotten out of bed yet today. If one of you could look—" She pulled the remainder of her words, then laughed. "After you've cleaned up."

"Sure," Arlo said, taking the hose from Layla and running it over his head. "Once we're both fit to be seen."

"She seems nice. Very protective of her elephants," Layla commented as Sylvie walked away.

"She is. And she's a good friend."

"Who will, hopefully, let me use her computer to order that chamomile tea. And some chocolate chips. When her assistant showed me in, I noticed they have a proper oven, so maybe she'll let me borrow it to bake cookies." Her eyes lit up. "You do still like them, don't you?"

"That was the one thing you made better than anyone else's." It was obvious the kiss wasn't going to be mentioned and, to be honest, there was no reason to. It had been a spontaneous moment. One that had happened naturally. So, really, what was there to say? They were adults. They didn't have to dwell on what had happened. And the likelihood of it happening again…

"Two days before you left, I baked three dozen. You ate every one of them in a matter of a couple of hours, which was my first clue that something bad was going to happen. You always turned to binge eating when something was about to come down on us. In retrospect, I should have realized that three dozen cookies meant it was going to be really bad."

"Better than taking out my frustrations in a bottle."

"Or we could have talked."

"Not really. By that time, I think we'd said everything that needed to be said. Rehashing what we couldn't have fixed wouldn't have gotten us anywhere." He finished hosing off the mud and handed the hose to Layla, who laid it in Tika's tub. "I mean, we already knew that neither of us would walk away with everything we wanted."

"I suppose toward the end we got into the habit of not talking because to do to that meant the problems didn't exist."

"Again, water under the bridge," he said "Anyway, rather than both of us staying here to take care of one patient, you stay and I'll head back to the clinic."

"I'd rather go," she said. "I scheduled a house call and it's on the way, so—"

* * *

Halfway back to the village, fighting to keep her mind on everything but Arlo, Layla noticed a cart up ahead. It was overturned, with a water buffalo standing off to the side of the road, still in its wooden yoke. Her heart jumped to her throat. There was a serious injury up ahead and she didn't have the means to do much more than apply a bandage. "Hello," she called out, wondering where the driver was. Hopefully gone off to get someone to help right his cart. "Does anybody need help? Can anybody hear me?"

She picked up her pace as something raised the hair on the back of her neck. "Is anybody hurt?" she yelled, once she was so close it startled the water buffalo, which scampered away.

Layla's first instinct took her from one side of the cart to the other, looking underneath where she could see something other than the grass, then looking at the corresponding ditch along the road, and even the field beyond that. At first she saw nothing, so she took another look around, approaching from the opposite direction. "Anybody here?" she yelled. "Please, if you can hear me, let me know where you are so I can help."

Stopping, she listened for a moment, then heard it. A faint voice, words she didn't understand. Even so, she recognized the sound of a person in dire trouble. So, once she got herself off the road and climbed waist-high into the ditch at the side of it, she managed to pull herself toward the front of the cart, and that's when she finally saw him. Or rather the small part of him that was exposed from mid-chest up. The grass there was so tall she'd missed him her first time around. Or maybe he'd been asleep or close to unconsciousness and hadn't heard her yell. But he had on her second attempt, and the first thing Layla did was take hold of his hand. Not for an assessment but to reassure him he wasn't alone.

"I'm going to help you," she said, not sure how she was going to do that. "I know you can't understand me but I'm going to do everything I know how to do to get you out of here." Then take him where? Back to the clinic that had nothing to repair the injuries she suspected he had sustained. "My name is *Doc* Layla. Can you tell me your name?"

He didn't answer but he squeezed her hand. "Good," she said. "You just hang in there with me."

Layla ripped some of the tall lemongrass from the ground and managed to clear an empty space for the man's head and shoulder, and she was shocked to see how young he was. Maybe thirty. At first glance he didn't appear to be bleeding. There was no seeming distress registering on his face. More like a look that said he couldn't believe this was happening to him.

"So far, I'm not seeing much," she said, coming up alongside him, then sitting down on the mound of dirt where she'd ripped out the grass. "But I'll keep looking." Because an overturned cart as heavy as this one had to have caused damage. To find it, she needed to be level with him to do an assessment. Underneath him would be dangerous, and there was nothing exposed on either side that would help her.

"Look, I know you've sustained some injuries, so I'm going to do my best to figure out what they are." Damn, she wished she knew the Thai translation for what she was telling him, but she didn't. "My name is Doc Layla," she said again, then pointed to herself. "Layla."

The young man responded with "Mongkut," which she took to be his name.

"I'm going to examine you, Mongkut," she said, pulling a stethoscope from her rucksack and hoping that he would identify that with doctor. And he did, as a look of relief washed over his scratched face.

What was under the cart, holding him in? Maybe with a little leverage he might be able to crawl out on his own, but until she knew more about what was going on, she couldn't risk it.

"I'm afraid I'm going to have to leave you where you are for a little while." If only she had something to give him for the pain. "The first thing I'm going to do is assess your vital signs: your heartbeat, breath sounds, blood pressure. I'm not sure I can see where, exactly, you're injured, but if you're stable enough, I'll run to the village and get some men to come lift the cart off you."

He listened intently, as if he understood every word, then when she finished speaking, he smiled at her and nodded his head in thanks.

Layla's first assessment was his blood pressure. She expected it to be elevated, considering the situation, and her face blanched when she couldn't hear it. Automatically, her hand went to his neck and her fingers to his carotid artery to find a pulse. It was there, but weak. Too weak. So she tried for another blood pressure reading and this time what she came up with was dangerously low, which led her to take a third reading that yielded the same result. That's when her heart started beating faster.

"I think you may have an injury I can't get to," she told Mongkut, as she removed Arlo's shirt and laid it across her patient's shoulders, like a thin layer of cloth was going to do any good. "So, try not to move while I do the rest of my tests."

Her mind raced with what to do with a crush

injury. She knew if Mongkut didn't receive aggressive medical treatment immediately, his chances of survival were very poor. "As I'm examining you, let me tell you what I think is happening," she said, knowing it was more for her own benefit than his. "Now I'm counting your respirations," she said, squeezing her hand inside the cramped space between Mongkut's body and the front rim of the cart to lay her hand on his chest. "Damn," she muttered. He was breathing too fast and too shallowly. "I think we have a bit of a problem here, Mongkut," she said. He roused when she said his name and forced a smile.

"First, there's hypovolemia. That's where you're bleeding internally, and it's nothing that is usually observable on the outside."

She listened to Mongkut's heart and the beat was off. Too slow, too labored, with some kind of arrhythmia she couldn't identify just from listening.

"The next thing that can happen is a cardiac arrhythmia, where the heart isn't beating correctly, and usually not pumping hard enough to distribute oxygen to all the places it needs to go."

She felt his carotid artery again and the pulse there was decidedly slower than it had been only moments earlier. But Mongkut was alert, still showing no outward signs of pain. Yet. Which was often the case when the body was shocked so drastically that the normal reactions weren't felt.

"Finally, we get to renal failure, meaning your kidneys shut down and the waste products start spreading through your body. Sometimes that takes a while, but if you've had a kidney injury, it can happen pretty fast."

She was glad he couldn't understand what she was saying because there was nothing good here. No help, no hospital, no treatment.

"Right now, you're not experiencing symptoms because, as your muscles are breaking down from a lack of oxygen, toxins are building up, getting ready to rush into your bloodstream. But the cart on top of you is acting like a dam, holding those toxins back. Keeping you alive."

Even though Mongkut couldn't understand her, she didn't have the heart to tell him what might happen once the cart came off.

"So, let's hope someone comes along pretty soon to help us." Optimistic words meant for her, not for Mongkut. "Because I'm sure you have a family at home waiting for you."

In her mind she saw a young wife, maybe a couple of young children, perhaps a baby. Sad images. Images she didn't want to have. Images that brought tears to her eyes that she tried hard to sniff back for fear he would see them then begin to sense what was really going on. She didn't want him to know. Not yet. Because if there was life, there was still hope. There had to be hope.

"And I'm not going to leave you, Mongkut," she said, automatically reaching over for the other carotid pulse, knowing the results before her fingers even touched his skin. "So, tell me about yourself," she said, even though that was impossible. But the sound of her voice was comforting to her, so she prayed it would be comforting to him as well. Especially as she struggled to sound upbeat. "Are you from around here?"

He must have guessed that to be a question, because he responded. His voice was weak, but he didn't sound scared, and she was grateful for that. As far as she knew, he was still feeling no pain, which, to almost everybody in his situation, meant nothing was wrong. "I'm originally from California, but my parents moved us to New York when I was young, and I loved our house..."

She looked up the road, hoping to see someone, but no one was coming. So she continued to hold his hand, feel for his pulse and talk—talk about anything. Because the words didn't matter. But being there with him—he needed to know he wasn't alone. Maybe that would ease his fear a little. Because it was beginning to show on his face.

So she talked, describing her house, the journeys she'd taken with her parents, the ups and downs of medical school and, after what seemed like an eternity, she finally heard a sputtering engine, one she recognized as Arlo's scooter. "Sounds like help is on the way," she said, stretching to look over the cart as Arlo came to a stop on the other side.

"Layla?" he cried, running over to her. "Are you hurt?"

She shook her head, fighting for control. "But Mongkut here is."

Arlo jumped down into the shallow ditch next to Layla, then smiled at the young man, who returned the smile. "What do we have?"

Layla swallowed hard before she said the awful words. "Crush injury."

"Are you sure?" Arlo asked, immediately grabbing Layla's stethoscope to listen to Mongkut's chest.

"I've been here fifteen or twenty minutes, and he's shifting down rapidly. Is there anything we can—?"

Arlo pulled the stethoscope off and handed it back to her. "Nothing," he said. "Not a damn thing."

She nodded, too afraid to speak for fear Mongkut would hear the discouragement in her voice. "So, what happens next?"

"He has a young wife and a baby daughter. His parents also live nearby as well. I think I need to bring them here. He needs them, and they should be with him when he..." He turned his head away. "Can you stay here with him, or do you want me to do that?"

"You know where his family is. You go."

"Are you sure?" Arlo asked, still looking away.

"I think you'd better hurry," she said. "I don't know how long he's been down, but I think it's been a while."

Arlo nodded then turned back to look at her, his eyes brimming with tears. "I'll be back as fast as I can." He pulled her close then hugged her. Then whispered, "I'm so sorry you have to do this."

His touch made her feel better. His kindness, his empathy... "Me, too," she said, wiping back tears. "It's the part about being a doctor I hate. The part I try to pretend doesn't exist until I can't pretend any longer."

With the back of his hand he also wiped away the tears streaming down her face, then kissed her lightly on the forehead. "I wish I could stay here with you, to take care of you and help you through it. You shouldn't have to do this alone."

"Neither should he." She looked down at Mongkut, whose eyes were shut now. "And there's really nothing left to do, is there?" She swallowed hard, as the man's breathing started to go agonal—a sort of gasping that happened just prior to death. "Get his family here, Arlo. Please..."

He nodded, then squeezed her hand, stood up and ran instead of getting on his scooter, which, at its top speed, was painfully slow, leaving Layla alone there, still holding Mongkut's hand. "He's gone to get your family. It shouldn't be long." And it wouldn't be. But she desperately hoped it would be long enough for his family to get here, to help him go on.

Mongkut smiled, then nodded as if he understood, and Layla wondered if somehow he did. "Anyway, let me tell you about the time in medical school when I—" She looked down at Mongkut, who was listening, but she noticed his eyelids starting to flutter. "You can't go to sleep," she said. "Your family's on the way, and you need to stay with me until they get here." She gave his hand a squeeze, but this time he didn't squeeze back. And his eyes finally fluttered shut. "I'm so sorry I couldn't fix it," she said, then stared off down the road, waiting for

Arlo to come back. Not letting go of Mongkut's hand, even though he was gone.

An hour later Arlo found Layla sitting in the dark, on the supply-closet floor. Not crying. Barely moving. "What can I do to help you through this?" he asked, sitting down next to her and pulling her into his arms.

"Sitting here like this is good. When I don't see anything around me, I can shut off my mind. Sometimes I have to do that—just shut down."

"What about feeling someone around you? Can you shut yourself off then?"

"I don't know," she said, honestly. She leaned her head into his shoulder. "I don't let myself get this involved, so I really don't know."

"You did everything you could," he said, sliding his arm around her. "His injury was too severe to fix."

"I knew that. But still…" She swatted at tears streaming down her face. "Sometimes there's just so much futility."

"Back when I was a resident, sometimes when I'd walk away from something I couldn't fix, I'd stand outside in the hall to collect myself before I turned myself loose on the world. Usually, I wanted to punch the wall. I still do, sometimes. Mentally, not physically—hands of a surgeon and all that. So I know what you're going through, Layla."

"You never told me that."

"Because I always wanted you to see me as better than I really was."

"I never saw anything but good in you, Arlo. Even though we had problems, I always thought you were an amazing man and an amazing surgeon."

"Thank you," he said, his voice almost a whisper. "That means a lot to me."

Layla sighed. "What we just did out there—I want to reframe it. I don't want to see it in my mind, but the darkness isn't pushing it away. And I'm not good at forgetting."

"Because you always think there's a way to make things different. Like with Mongkut. His destiny was sealed before you got there, but you helped him. He wasn't alone at the end. You were there, holding his hand. It's a good thing, Layla. Nothing that needs reframing. And I'm so proud of the way you took care of him even when you knew…"

"I'm glad you're here now. You always took good care of me in the bad moments. I liked that. Got spoiled by that."

"I didn't know."

"Because I didn't tell you. What was the point? What was the point in telling you a lot of things? You weren't going to stay. You weren't going to be a real part of my life. I always hoped holding back would keep me from getting hurt in the end."

"Did it?"

"No. I liked us—together. Loved us together. Loved you, Arlo. I loved you."

"But you loved your independence more."

"I needed that independence to survive. Did I love it more? I don't know. Maybe at the time I did because I was struggling so hard to find out who I was. And there was you—the rock-solid man who'd found himself long before we'd met. I wanted to be what you were, Arlo. But I wasn't at a place in my life yet where I could make that happen. All I knew from life was that if it didn't turn out the way I thought it should, it would break my heart. So I really didn't embrace the opportunities I had."

She started to relax against him. "Living large, as they call it. That's what's always frightened me most. I didn't know how to do it because everything I had was handed to me. I'd never had to work hard for anything, and I didn't know how. Which made me hide behind a wall of independence that would have crumbled in a slight breeze had it ever really been tested. It was a façade, Arlo. And I was a fake."

"So even now you hold yourself back. Shut

yourself in the dark and pretend the scary things don't exist."

"Sometimes it works."

"And now?" He tilted her face toward his. "Is it working now, Layla?"

Rather than responding, she reached over and ran her hand through his curly hair. Then she kissed him. Thoughtfully, deeply. Urgently. Once, twice, until every pore in his body was filled with longing, and every nerve-ending in his mouth tingled. Harder, deeper, with a need he'd never felt in her before. "Should we stop?" he whispered, pulling back from her, but only slightly. He hoped she would say no, hoped that she would insist on continuing. But this was Layla, and she was not predictable. Not in anything they'd ever had between them.

"Do you want to?" she asked.

He had no will to tell her no, but answered her with his lips pressed to her cheek, causing her to shiver so hard he could feel her body tremble. "I can. Right now..." He brushed the hollow of her temple. "Or now." Next, he brushed kisses to the line of her cheekbone then continued down to her throat, her shoulder, finally nuzzling his way into the top of her breast. "Tell me, Layla. Because I won't stop if you don't."

Again, she said nothing, but she did knot her fists against his chest, then slowly, very slowly splayed them open and pulled him hard against her. Arlo groaned softly, a low growl in his throat almost, then circled his arms, pulling her on top of him. As he slid down to the floor from his sitting position, she slid with him, on top. And they rolled over to let him take the top position, still tangled together, still kissing. Then she reached up, ran her fingers through his hair once again, something she'd always done, something he'd always loved, and she finally spoke. "No, don't stop."

"You're a damn good doctor, Layla. A damned good surgeon. People with your skills don't come along that often, so why give up everything you've worked so hard to accomplish only to become what my grandfather is—a great administrator who's been away from patient care so long he'd be a detriment if he stepped back in. Is that what you really want for yourself? To keep yourself hidden away from your true talent?"

It was evening now, and they were sitting on the front step of the hospital, eating bowls of sticky rice and fruit. What had happened in the closet—they hadn't spoken of it. It had been a brief moment in time, a little bit of history repeating itself, and Layla was afraid to think past that, afraid because she wanted more, but she didn't trust herself enough to believe that she could ever be enough for Arlo. She wanted to be, but her only real confidence was in her ambition and not in what she truly wanted.

Maybe because the one thing she'd always wanted—her parents' respect—had always been refused her. They were excited now that she was finally advancing. Showing more interest in her now than ever before. And in a life where she'd futilely tried to earn their respect, she was afraid to walk away from the sure path. "What if administration is my true talent?"

"What if patient care is?"

"Here, in the jungle, like what you do?"

"Anywhere you want, Layla. You just don't trust yourself enough." Arlo took her bowl and set it down, then took her hand and pulled her up off the step. "I want to show you something."

Rather than heading through the village, they turned away from it and walked, hand in hand, down a moonlit dirt path until they came to a pool of water. In the glow, she could see it was surrounded by massive boulders. And she could hear night sounds: birds and monkeys. Maybe even Chauncy, looking for his lady love. It was a beautiful place, filled with such peace she didn't even think about the snakes or the other things she feared. With Arlo, she was safe.

"See that rock?" he said, pointing to a large

round boulder sitting just at the water's edge. "Let me help you up there."

"Why?" she asked, as he pulled her in that direction.

He didn't answer, though. Instead, he bent to give her a foothold, and there she was, sitting atop a boulder and trusting Arlo enough to simply experience the moment without her usual doubt or fear.

"Now stand up," he urged, reaching up to hold her hand as she did so. "And shout, 'I am strong.'"

She hesitated for a moment, not because she didn't want to do as he instructed but because this was a perfect place, a perfect moment and she didn't want that to change.

"Do it, Layla," he urged. "I am strong."

Smiling, she nodded. Then drew in her breath and shouted, "I am strong." And her voice echoed back to her. *Strong...strong... strong...strong.* For an instant the monkey chatter stopped, and the birds went silent, and all she could hear were her words. "I am strong," she whispered. Then she shouted again. "I am strong." *Strong...strong...strong.* And closed her eyes to take in only her voice. *Her voice.* Nobody else's.

"You always have been," Arlo said. "You just never knew that."

She smiled down at him but didn't speak as there were no words to say to the man who'd just given her the world.

CHAPTER SEVEN

"KANYA BANLENGCHIT HAS asked us to take the evening meal with her and her family tonight. She has three small children, so they eat early—if you're interested."

They'd spent the day working, going in different directions, passing each other on the road occasionally, but only long enough to wave or say hello. It was good. He liked the hard work, and watching Layla throw herself into things like he'd never seen her do before made him happy. She was actually smiling each time they met up. Smiling, enjoying her work, anxious to get on to the next patient.

It didn't surprise him that they worked so well together. They shared the same ethic, the same skill. But they'd always been beaten by their different destinations. Not so now. Even though they weren't together, they also weren't apart.

Layla, who was stretched out on her cot with Chauncy, raised herself up to look at him. "Tell her I appreciate the offer, but I'm really exhausted. I don't know when I have ever worked so hard."

"Did you enjoy it?"

She laughed. "If I admit that I did, are you going to tease me about all the times I told you I would hate it?"

His eyes crinkled into a smile. "Probably."

"Have you no pity for the doctor with blisters on her feet?"

"Aloe vera is a good cure for that and, as it happens, several of the ladies here grow it in their gardens."

Layla's response was to moan. "And if I tell you my leg muscles ache, you'll tell me to eat more magnesium-rich foods, then run out and pick me some bananas."

"Thailand does have about a hundred different varieties."

She sat her tea cup aside and dropped back onto her pillows. Chauncy got up from his spot at the end of the cot to investigate what was left in the cup. "Raincheck?"

"Food's been cooking all day. People will be offended."

"So how long before I have to go?"

"Right now," he said, with the most innocent of all smiles she'd ever seen on him crossing his face.

"And when were you supposed to have told me?"

"This morning."

She sat back up, then climbed off the cot. This reminded her of some of their dates. He'd make the reservations then forget to tell her until the last minute. Or he'd accept a party invitation then tell her about it thirty minutes after they were supposed to arrive. Typical Arlo. Actually, she'd gotten used to this and found it almost endearing. Almost. "I'll be ready in twenty. After my shower."

"Dinner's in ten, before your shower."

"You look like you've just stepped out of the shower."

"I did. Ten minutes ago."

She grabbed a towel and some clean clothes from her stack, and brushed past him. "Like I said, twenty minutes. And next time..." She stopped, and mussed his still-wet curly hair. "Give me some warning."

"When I warned you, it took you an hour. Just consider this as my way of saving some time."

"And just consider this as my way of saying thirty minutes now, instead of twenty."

He chuckled as she walked out the door, then threw himself down on the cot. "Don't know about you, Chauncy, but I still can't figure out what women are about."

Kanya put on quite a spread, and Layla savored every bite she took. Unfortunately for her tummy, she took too many of those bites, drank way too much of the various fruit juices and by the end of the meal felt like she wouldn't eat again for days. "Tell her this was amazing," she said to Arlo, who was sitting on a mat across from her. "And that I don't think I've ever eaten so much at any one sitting in my life."

"She'll take that as a compliment. Oh, and there's more. A papaya pudding. It's served a while after the meal to help with digestion."

"Well, I think I'm going to need more help than simple papaya can give me." She watched the children take platters and bowls away from the tables. Dozens of them. "Why so much?" she asked Arlo. "Most of the other meals I've had here are simple. And this…"

"It's a hero's meal. Everyone in the village contributed. That's why there was so much of it—you received what would probably be several days' worth of it for several families. And Kanya was the one to prepare and serve it because Mongkut was her cousin."

"But I'm not a hero. I didn't…" She swallowed hard. "Why would they do this with the way it turned out?"

"It's a traditional way to feed someone important, and what you did yesterday earned you that distinction, even though you probably think you didn't earn it. It's high praise, Layla. It means you're one of them now."

"Even though I couldn't save him?" She waved to a group of women on the front porch who were simply standing there, looking in.

"You stayed with him, Layla. Held his hand. Talked to him. To the people here, that shows great bravery. And compassion. So, like it or not, you're stuck with that reputation."

"I'm…humbled. For all these people to embrace me this way…" Tears welled in her eyes. "Why didn't you say something? Tell me what this was about?"

"Because when you live here, spontaneity is a good thing. I know you've always liked to keep to your rigid schedule, but that's not the way everybody lives their life. And wasn't it fun to just let go and have a good time without overthinking it all day?"

"I do overthink, don't I?"

"Only when you're not sleeping." He smiled, took her hand and kissed the back of it. "You *are* strong, Layla, and you *do* fit in wherever you want to."

She looked at all the people huddling in and outside the hut, talking, laughing, having a good time. "I want to fit in, Arlo. I really do." Somewhere. Anywhere. Here?

It was well into the night when they finally left, after eating leftovers. And Layla was so stuffed and lethargic she was practically hanging onto Arlo, letting him drag her. She'd watched him tonight. Playing with the children. Strumming a guitar and singing. Listening patiently to incessant chatter. Mixing. Mingling. Laughing. Being part of everything. "Is there anything you don't do?" she asked, her admiration overflowing as they entered the hut.

"Besides cooking? Let me think…" He was laughing as he led her to her side of the curtain then went back around to his own side.

Arlo was one of those men who was too good to be true. The kind a woman would fall for in a heartbeat, provided it was a woman who wanted to share his lifestyle. She could see why he didn't want to change it. This was where he fit. Perfectly. "I'm waiting," she called out, too tired to change into her night clothes.

"And I'm still thinking."

"Maybe start with humility?"

"No. I'm good at being humble."

"Is there such a thing as being too humble to be honestly humble?"

"And you're implying, what?"

"That you're a good man, Arlo. A very good man." Words said as her eyes closed.

On the other side of the curtain, Arlo simply sat cross-legged on his mat, wondering what this was about. They'd had a good evening—maybe one of the best they'd ever had and, for now, that was enough. And what she'd said about him as she'd drifted off left him feeling curious. Good, but curious. Telling him he was a good man was nice. Telling him he was sexy would have been better. Telling him he was the man she'd always wanted would have been the best. But for now he'd settle for good.

"Doc Arlo," someone outside whispered through the mosquito netting. "Dusit—" The woman out there started explaining something even Arlo couldn't comprehend, she was talking so fast. But he knew what this was about. One of his problem patients. Another late-night call because Dusit always seemed to manifest his symptoms in the middle of the night.

As he grabbed up his medical bag and slid into his sandals, he thought about waking Layla to let her know where he'd be, because these calls to Dusit could run into a couple hours or more. But he hated to disturb her, especially since her sleep patterns were so sporadic to begin with. So he slipped out of the hut and headed off in the direction of the main part of the village, and veered to a side road, hesitating before he approached the house as he really wasn't in the mood for this. Acute patients were one thing. So were chronic patients who worked to take care of themselves. But Dusit was neither. He was a chronic who relied on Arlo too much and did nothing to help himself. And there wasn't much he could do about it.

So, sucking in a deep breath, he proceeded up the front walk until he reached the wooden porch where Dusit Chaichanatham was sitting, eating slices of mango.

"Doc Arlo," the man said, grinning and offering a slice to Arlo.

Dusit was a diabetic with blood sugar so out of control that he was a constant worry for any number of side effects. He was a street vendor in the village who specialized in selling *khanom*—sweets—and he ate too many of his own sweets to be healthy. His weight had ballooned at an alarming rate shortly after he'd turned forty. Plus, he was suffering leg cramps and blurry vision.

"Good evening, Dusit," he said, approaching the front porch. "Are you always hungry this late at night?"

His answer was to down another piece and grin. "Very good," he said.

"How many do you eat before you go to bed?"

He held up fingers to indicate three. Not good. A mango contained considerably more sugar than most fruits. And while they were easy to come by out here, they weren't always the best choice in eating, unless in moderation.

"Do you eat anything else before bed?" he asked, sitting down next to the rotund man on a wooden bench. It creaked under Arlo's added weight, so he decided to stand back up before their combined weight broke it.

"*Khanom chan*," he said, still grinning as mango juice dripped off his chin. A layered coconut dessert.

"Seriously? And is there anything else?" Arlo asked, pretty sure he really didn't want to know.

"*Kao tom mud*," he said. A sweet sticky rice made from black beans, tamarind, bananas and coconut milk. A very sweet dish indeed. "*Itim kati*." An ice cream made entirely of coconut milk because many people in Thailand suffered from lactose intolerance. "*Tuang muan sot*." He patted his belly with that one, which told Arlo the soft, sweet pancake made from coconut and sesame seeds was one of his favorites. "*Sang kaya fug tong*." Essentially, pumpkin custard filled with a sweet cream.

All of it sounded good, and for poor Dusit deadly. "Anything else?" Arlo asked, suddenly realizing that this man's diet consisted mainly of the sweets he sold for a living.

"*Tong yord.*"

Arlo moaned with that one as it was an excessively sweet dessert made from egg yolk, sugar, rice flour and jasmine water. Did this man ever eat anything healthy?

"Well, I know you haven't been feeling well, and it may have something to do with your eating habits, like I've told you before." If it didn't, he'd burn his medical credentials and spend the rest of his life washing elephants. "So, what's your complaint tonight?"

"Blurry head. Tingly. Some dizzy."

"Does your lower back hurt?" Arlo asked, indicating the area on both sides of his own back that contained the kidneys.

Dusit shook his head.

"And your feet?"

"Good feet," Dusit said.

"Well, you know what I have to do." He grabbed a blood sugar monitor from his bag. "I know you don't like this, and that you usually refuse, but if you're feeling poorly enough to have your wife come and get me in the middle of the night, I've got to test your sugar level." It was always high, even with insulin shots, which

Dusit normally refused as he was deathly afraid of needles. "Let me swab your finger and we'll get this over quickly."

"But no shots," Dusit warned.

"No promises."

"Then no finger." He curled his fingers into a fist.

"No finger, then I have to close your vendor stall down since I am the health officer here, and I believe your sweets are harming you." Over the course of time he'd tried all manners of persuasion, but threatening the man with taking away his livelihood, which he wouldn't do, was the one that worked. And sure enough—one chubby finger popped out of his fist and he stuck it out for Arlo.

The draw was quick, and shortly the meter registered a whopping blood sugar count of five hundred and seventy-five. Normal ranged between eighty and one hundred and twenty.

"It's a problem, Dusit. I can give you a shot to bring it down, but you've got to change the way you eat. And get some exercise."

The man was always either sitting or reclining. He didn't even have to walk to work since his stall was in his front yard. Truth was, Arlo was running out of patience here, as well as fresh out of ideas that might work for Dusit.

Maybe Layla could try something different. Fresh eyes on a problem never hurt.

"So tonight it's a pretty big shot. And I'd suggest you quit eating now for the insulin to work."

Dusit huffed out an impatient sigh. "No good letting food waste."

"And no good trying to eat it all because, eventually, that's going to kill you. We've had that talk many times, Dusit. You know what's ahead of you." He filled a syringe with insulin, totally hating how much Dusit required, then indicated for the man to drop his trousers, and when he did so, Arlo jabbed him in the thigh. Dusit's response was to scream so loud and long that the lights from homes all around the area came on. "You may have to have another one in a while," Arlo said, dropping the used syringe into a disposable sharps container he carried in his bag. "I'll be back in a while to check, or I'll be sending my colleague."

"No lady doc," Dusit protested.

"It's not your choice, Dusit. If you cooperate with me, it can become your choice. But until then it's my choice." And he hoped Layla did have something in her bag of medical tricks for Dusit as the man was an eating, breathing stroke waiting to happen.

By the time Arlo was halfway back to the hut,

he ran into Layla, who was running in his direction, carrying her medical bag. "Several people reported hearing screaming, so I—"

He waved her off with his hand. "Just an uncooperative patient showing me how uncooperative he can really be."

"Seriously? He woke half the village."

"Man doesn't like needles."

"You had to give him a shot."

"Either that or watch him mango himself to death right before my very eyes." He looked up at the dark sky and blew out a frustrated breath. "He's a serious diabetic. Has vision problems, early onset neuropathy and God only knows what else, since he refuses a physical. He's on my insulin rounds in the morning, but he won't take insulin. And to make matters worse, he's the sweets vendor, and he eats all the leftovers. So—any suggestions?"

"What have you tried?"

"Everything. Talking, educating, reasoning, threatening. Showing him pictures of what his complications can turn into if he's not careful." He reached out and took hold of Layla's hand as they headed back home. "He doesn't respond to anything."

"Some patients won't be helped, Arlo. We both know that."

"He's forty, Layla. Just a few years older than

me. And he has young children. They don't deserve to have their daddy die by the time he's forty-five. But I don't know what else to do."

"Would he listen to me?"

"Probably not."

"Could I try?"

"Absolutely. But don't expect much. Dusit's the very definition of stubborn pride."

"And you sound exhausted," she said as they trudged up the wooden steps to their hut.

"I am. Sometimes I wish—"

She laid a finger to his lips to silence him. "Sometimes we all wish we'd made other choices. But you were meant to be here, Arlo, and Dusit's not going to defeat you."

"How did you know that's where I was going?"

"Because I know you, and I know had badly you take it when one of your patients doesn't respond. So..." She stood on tiptoe and kissed him gently on the lips. "Go to sleep and we'll deal with your problem patient in the morning. Oh, and take the cot. Tonight I think you need it more than I do." She brushed his cheek with her thumb, then crossed the room to his mat and lay down there.

For the life of him, there were times when he couldn't figure out why he'd walked away from her. Tonight was one of them.

* * *

"He actually came here for his shot," Arlo said, a towel wrapped around his middle and another around his head. "Before I was awake."

He was so distracting, almost naked that way, but she couldn't force her gaze anywhere else. "That's because we had a little talk and I told him if he didn't work harder and make it easier for you to take care of him, we might have to take him to hospital and leave him there for a while until they got his diabetes under control. Mind you, he was eating some pastry when we talked, but he did promise to come for his shot, and I'm glad to hear he did."

"So, where have you been?" He turned his back to her, dropped his towel and pulled on his underpants, then his cargos. No care in the world that he was flashing his bare bum at her. A bare bum she'd always admired.

"Doing your early rounds. You were so exhausted I decided to let you sleep."

He tossed the towel from his head into a hamper with the rest of the towels, then finger-combed his curls. She used to love doing that. Running her fingers through his hair. Massaging around his eyes. Kissing his neck—his neck, maybe the sexiest part of him. She'd loved to nibble his neck.

"I appreciate that. I can't remember the last time I got to sleep in. It was nice. Thank you."

She smiled. "That's what partners are for."

But partners in what sense? Could she mean what he was thinking about? Nah. While she was committed to doing a good job here, she wasn't focused on anything other than her promotion. So many things had changed about Layla, but so many hadn't. That's something he'd have to come to terms with or else this time, when she walked away, it would be far worse than last time. Because last time his feelings had been practice feelings. He recognized that now. But this time…his feelings were deeper. Much, much deeper. And there was no practice to them as they were the real thing. Last time he'd had wounds. This time, if he let it get away from him, he would have permanent scars.

After a busy morning, Arlo was ready to take a break by midday. Normally he worked straight through, but he'd been thinking about his mother all morning. The work she'd done here. The happiness her life had brought her, and how it had shone on her face. The low moments when she'd thought about Eric. She had been the embodiment of civilized when so much around her hadn't been. Like Layla. Strong, determined and yet gentle in ways she hadn't often shown.

He liked what was coming out in Layla. Nothing was overt. Everything was subtle. But she now carried candy for the children. And she smiled. Maybe that was the best part—her beautiful smile that simply seemed to come more naturally now.

"Care to go get something to eat with me?" he asked as she strolled into their hut only moments after he did. He was seated on the floor, reclining in a pile of pillows. She kept her distance, standing across the dim room. But her arms weren't folded across her chest, the way they were so much of the time. In fact, she looked casual. At ease with herself and her surroundings—something he'd never seen very often in her. It was nice. Dangerous since it gave him crazy ideas that simply had no place between them. But nice all the same.

"I'd sit with you for tea, but half the food vendors in the village were offering me samples today." She patted her belly. "Apparently, I have no will power."

Arlo laughed. "The village does have its charms."

"And calories. Lot and lots of calories."

"Like you have to worry about that." Her body was perfect, and she was one of the lucky ones who could eat everything in sight and not gain an ounce. Back when they'd been together, he had been the one who'd had to watch himself. Now it didn't matter so much as he was so physically active most of the time.

"But it catches up to you. My mother—the svelte, beautiful actress—has been hating life lately because she's put on some pounds."

"If I recall, on the couple times I met her she was very…nice."

"We all change as we get older. For my mom, it's her weight. For my dad, it's his hairline."

"And for you?"

Frowning, Layla thought for a moment. "I'm here. I think that's a huge change."

"But would you be here if there wasn't something substantial in it for you?"

"Probably not. I do like my material world. Maybe not the way I used to. I mean, I don't own fifty pairs of shoes now. But a nice warm shower, a comfortable bed without mosquito netting—my needs are much simpler, but they're still my needs. So, let me ask you what changes you've seen in yourself."

"I think I'm more aware, and tolerant, of people's needs and differences."

"You *were* pretty rigid."

"It was a brave new world out there for me. I was afraid of getting lost in it. I think it's easier to be who you really are when you're where you belong." He pushed himself off the floor, then headed for the door. But before he even got to the shoe rack, someone outside was yelling. "Bleeding bad. Come help."

Layla immediately ran to the door and there, in the street, was a panicked woman who was covered in blood. She was explaining something to Arlo. It took her the length of time it took him to put on his sandals, then he ducked back in the hut. "Bad one," he said. "Grab your bag and follow her. I've got to run over to the hospital and get..." he swallowed. "...my amputation kit."

"What?" Layla sputtered.

"I'm not really sure. But it has something to do with someone caught in a tree, who's bleeding to death. She—his wife—said his leg won't come out."

Layla nodded, her whole body suddenly feeling numb. "Maybe it's not as bad—" She bit back the rest of her words, grabbed her medical kit and ran outside, only to be passed by Arlo, who was on his way to the hospital. They met up, moments later, down the road. "I've never done an amputation," she said. "If that's what this is about."

"Neither have I." Which meant they were going blind into this. But blind together. While it didn't improve the situation, it did make him feel much better that Layla would be the one there to help him.

In the full light of a bright day she could see the drying blood on the woman's clothing. A lot of it. And ahead, where a crowd was gathering, a man tied into a tree. Bleeding. Tied off so he wouldn't fall. *But in a tree.*

"We can't do anything while he's up there," she said to Arlo.

"Unless we can't get him down with his leg intact." He pulled away from Layla, then went to talk to the wife, Naiyana, who was already back under the tree, dropped to her knees and crying, as several women were trying to comfort her. She truly wished she understood the language and vowed that for the rest of her time here she'd work hard on learning more of it. Because, if not for Arlo, she was not sure what she'd do.

"He was cutting a branch of a tree. It was hanging too close to their house, obstructing the light, so he went up to cut it down and somehow—and I don't understand more than the gist of this—it fell back on him, crushing part of his leg, and he can't get loose of it. A couple of the men went up to see what they could do, and decided he needed medical attention, so they tied him into the tree to make sure he wouldn't fall out. Naiyana said there's lots of blood and she thinks he might be dying."

"Is he conscious?" Layla asked, coming up to the ladder still leaning against the tree, then looking up at her patient—who wasn't moving.

"I'm not sure. Possibly fading in and out, according to Naiyana. Apparently, he was delirious earlier. Nothing he said was making sense."

"So..." This wasn't sounding good. And from the look on Arlo's face she knew he felt the same way. Which scared her as she thought of him as almost fearless, able to handle any situation, while she was completely helpless trying to climb a tree. Then getting stuck or, worse, falling out of it. He didn't need two emergencies to deal with, but her hands were shaking. So were her knees. And she was sweating like a genteel lady would never dare to sweat.

"I'll go up first and get myself on that big limb right above him. If I tie myself on, I can reach down and help you. The amputation, if that's what it comes to."

Now her heart was beginning to race, and she feared a panic attack was coming. She was deathly afraid of heights and trees. That one serious fall when she'd been a kid, two surgeries, and three weeks in a hospital and rehab—all that might have been the reason she'd become a doctor. But that wasn't registering right now. The only thing that was registering was climbing a tree and amputating a leg. "Why can't you—?"

"Because I need to be able to help lower him down. In this situation my strength is needed more than my medical skill."

She looked up again, swallowed hard. "I'm not sure I can climb up there, Arlo. You know how I am about—"

"You'll be safe, I promise," he said, putting a steadying arm around her shoulder. "No falling out of the tree like you did when you were eight, and no broken leg for you this time." Pulling her closer, he leaned down and whispered, "I'd never put you in danger, Layla. *Never.*"

"I know that. But still..." She shook her head. "I'm afraid I won't be able to...perform, even if I do manage to get up there." She could almost feel herself falling to the ground. The few seconds of wild fear when her brain wouldn't function, then hitting hard, and a jolt so paralyzing that she couldn't breathe. Then the pain. The excruciating pain and the fear that her parents might not care. Even though it had happened when she'd been only a little girl, she felt like that little girl now. Except this time she had Arlo, and she trusted him with everything inside her. "But I'll try."

"Don't force yourself," he whispered. "I don't want anything happening to you."

She managed a weak smile. "Neither do I." Then melted when he bent to kiss her cheek. "I can do this, Arlo. Remember? I am strong!" Brave words she desperately needed to be true, because too many things in life scared her. Being with Arlo, being without him—she couldn't let the practice of her medicine become one of those fears. "I am strong," she whispered. Then turned to face Arlo. "I am. I really am."

"You are," Arlo agreed, then started up the ladder, leaving her standing underneath her patient, going over the procedure in her mind as her hands began to steady. "Get up there, get myself secured, do my job." She repeated that out loud several times as she walked round and round the tree, surveying the emergency scene from every angle as Arlo got himself secured. "Just do my job." And she could, because Arlo believed in her. For the first time she felt that belief. It was palpable. And it braced her for what she had to do.

"Somewhere in medical school I think they forgot to teach us how to do this," she said as she reached the top of the ladder and slung her leg over the sturdy branch where her patient was dangling, unconscious now, on the far end. "And if I ever open my own medical school…"

She began to slide, inch by inch, to the end of the limb.

"Another ambition?" Arlo asked. He was mere feet above her, currently tying himself to the tree trunk.

"Right now, my only ambition is to get this over with and get our patient out of the tree." She inched a little more, then stopped.

"Tie yourself to the trunk, Layla," Arlo said.

"If I do, I won't be able to reach him." She leaned forward, just enough that her fingers could asses the pulse in his neck. "It's pretty weak, Arlo. I don't think we have much time." She moved forward a little more. "What can you see from up there?"

"His leg is stuck in a fork. It's swollen so badly it won't come loose without—"

"And my best position to do that from down here?"

"Another few inches forward, Layla. But be careful."

"Will the branch hold my weight?"

"Virote's weight—that's his name—is pretty evenly dispersed between the limbs, so you'll be good. And since he's basically just flat on his back and not really hanging, that will simplify things for you."

"Nothing's going to simplify things, Arlo. I'm a doctor's who has never done an amputation, and my first is in a tree." She looked up at him, managed a weak smile. "Remember when I was talking about creature comforts? Well, this isn't one of them."

Layla managed to move herself several more inches and that's when she was finally able to get a good look at Virote's leg. The fracture was compound, and bits of bone were shattered and littering his wound. And the bleeding—it was steady. Not profuse but coming hard enough that he would bleed out shortly if they didn't get it stopped. And the only way to do that—

"He already has a partial amp to the leg," she said, applying the tourniquet above the wound to stop the bleeding. "And now..." She shook her head and gritted her teeth. This was the moment when everything she'd ever learned as a doctor would be put to the test.

"Is he secured, in case he comes to?" Arlo asked. He was on his belly now, leaning as far down as he could and still be safe.

"I've just given him a shot, doubled the medication dose, which is the best I can do." Yet, she still feared they could all fall out of the tree if Virote woke up and started to fight.

"Take care of yourself, Layla. And if, for any reason, you get dizzy, or anything puts you at risk, get out of there. I know we've got to treat our patient, but we've also got to keep ourselves from getting hurt. And I don't want anything happening to you. Do you understand?"

Layla nodded as she opened up the amputation kit while Arlo, above her, prepared ropes to lower Virote to the ground once he was free of the tree. "Same goes for you. Keep safe, Arlo. Oh, and about that tea we were going to have—raincheck?"

Her first move to help Virote was to pack as much gauze around the wound as she could without compromising her surgical field. And even out on a tree limb, that's what it was. A surgical field. Then she did a quick assessment of his vital signs. "Blood pressure low," she said, taking the reading off the wrist monitor she'd managed to get on him. "Pulse weak and too rapid," she continued. "Also, he's trying to talk but he's beginning to perseverate." Repeat the same words over and over. Likewise, he was beginning to trail off some of his words in guttural animal-type sounds. Sure signs of rapid deterioration.

Arlo shouted something to the people below, and several men turned and ran back to the village. "They're going to get more rope so we can make a sling to lower him when it's done, so—it's time, Layla."

She swallowed hard against the lump that was forming in her throat. Even though Arlo was close. Still, knowing he was there, looking down at everything she did, made things better. So, first, she took out the scalpel to initiate the procedure, then cleaned the area with alcohol wipes—not that it made much difference considering how dirty the wound was—then proceeded with cutting through skin, muscle and tendons. But halfway through the procedure the scalpel broke, and Arlo gasped from above. The setback lasted only a couple of seconds as she looked through the kit to see what else she could use. Then she saw them. A pair of trauma shears. And they worked beautifully. Got her through this part of the procedure without a hitch.

"OK," she said to Arlo. "First part's done. Moving on to the second."

"You're doing great," he said.

"And you are so going to owe me a nice dinner in Bangkok before I go home," she retorted, then lurched backward as Virote began to stir. Quickly she drew up another shot of medication and gave it to him—a much bigger dose than she would have liked, but safety was as important up here as the actual procedure. And, luckily, little by little, Virote settled down again. "And if he needs much more to keep him sedated, I'm afraid you're going to have to sing him a lullaby because I've already given him much more than I'm comfortable with."

"Can't sing without my guitar."

"Then you stay here, while I go back to the hut and find it." She checked Virote's eyes and blood pressure. "He's gone again, so let's get this over with. When I get done here, he's going to be all yours to manage because there's nothing I can do to help get him down from this angle. So, are you ready, because I'm going to do this fast." As much for her sake as for Virote's.

"The question is, are *you* ready?"

"I have to be, don't I?" Layla grabbed forceps to clamp the skin and other tissue back from the worst part of the wound and also create a tunnel under the bone, which would allow for better access. Then next use the bone saw.

She wiped the sweat from her face before she started that part of the procedure. Normally, one of her surgical attendants did that, but this was surgery at its rawest, something no doctor could ever anticipate doing, and it was all up to her. Suddenly, all the respect she'd felt she'd never had didn't matter anymore. She had the skill. That's what counted. "I am strong," she whispered, then commenced.

"His vitals are still bad," Layla said to Arlo. He was driving her SUV while she tended her patient. The procedure had gone as well as could be expected, and with the assistance of several villagers Arlo had been able to give Virote a smooth ride to the ground. But the poor man needed more surgery to repair what she'd cut. And they were on their way to the regional hospital where he would be treated for his shock symptoms and stabilized enough to transport him to a public hospital in Bangkok for the next surgery.

"He's lucky to be alive," Arlo said, glancing in the rear-view mirror to see Layla applying another dressing to the still-bleeding wound. "But he's going to need a lot of volume replacement," he commented. Blood transfusion.

"And this is just the beginning of it. After his next surgery, and he's fitted for a prosthesis..."

Arlo interrupted her. "That probably won't happen for quite a while. If ever."

"What? Why not?"

"That's just the way it is. The public hospital will take care of keeping him alive, and even getting him started on some rehab. In other words, living life as an amputee. But for a prosthesis perseverate the waiting lists are long. Where he should be fitted in six to eight weeks, it'll take twice that long, or more. He'll have good care in the interim, but nothing about it will be speedy."

Layla leaned back against the SUV door and shut her eyes. "Seriously?"

"Like I keep telling you, that's the way it is here, Layla. One of the reasons I stay. Even if I can't provide them the best medical care, given my limitations, I can do something. If we hadn't been here to help him today, the villagers would have attempted something that would have killed him. Or he'd have stayed in that tree until he bled to death. When you live in the jungle, things don't come easy. But there are people like my parents, and me, who do the best we can with what we have. And that's another thing you should address in *your* medical school. The differences in medical care around the world."

"I guess I've been too sheltered, because before I came here, I didn't know… Well, I didn't know pretty much any of this."

"Neither did my parents. A lot of their motivation to come here was to get away from the threats Eric's dad was making. But look at what they did. They became these amazing nomadic doctors who made such a huge difference, which gives me the chance to make a difference as well. They were pioneers in a sense. And it turned into a life they loved with a passion."

She reached across the back of his seat and brushed his cheek. "It's good," she said. "What you do—all good. I'm glad the people here have you." And in so many ways she wished she could have him, too. But could she be the partner he needed? Not in the relationship sense so much as the medical? Could she be to Arlo what his mother had been to his father? Life partners with a common goal?

Arlo knew her as the girl who required fifty pairs of shoes to make her happy and, in so many ways, that's who she had been back when they'd been together and, in a sense, even after she'd come here. Not in the literal sense, of course. But being away from that life made that life she'd lived seem so frivolous. Inconsequential. But could he see past what she'd been, and truly look at what she was becoming? Or was he too stuck in their past to see anything more than what she'd always shown him?

"Well, it's not the prettiest view, but it's the best I could find at a moment's notice." Arlo placed two wrapped sandwiches and a bottle of wine on the stone wall surrounding the garden and reflecting pool, then sat down next to her. “Virote just came out of surgery and he’s doing well.”

They hadn’t left the regional hospital yet. Partly because they wanted to see their emergency through to the end and partly because they were both exhausted. Not fit for the long drive back. “It’s been a while since I’ve heard city sounds,” she said, not interested in the food as much as simply sitting here with Arlo, relaxing. “All those horns, and this isn’t even a big city.”

“Just think what it would be like in Bangkok.” He uncorked the wine, which he’d bought at a little market down the street, and poured it into two glasses, not stemware but sturdy hospital glasses.

“I was there for a day before I came out to your hospital. It was…nice. So many things to see and do. But I think I prefer jungle sounds.”

He choked, laughing. “Seriously? You’re turning into Layla of the jungle?”

“Maybe. I don’t know. Probably not.”

“Now that’s a solid answer, if I ever did hear one.”

“I like the people, Arlo. And the challenge of the medicine, even though I’ve complained about it. It makes me feel alive in a way I’ve never felt alive before. I think I’ll miss it when I go home.”

"You're really going back to that?"

"It's who I am. At least, who I know me to be." She took a sip of the wine, then looked up at the stars. Beautiful dots of twinkling diamonds set against a black backdrop. "Do you think I could take some of that with me?"

"I think you can have whatever you want, Layla. Your heart's desire, if your heart is involved." He pulled her to her feet and into his embrace. "Do you remember the nights we'd sit outside on the balcony and just…breathe?"

"Those were nice nights, Arlo. Sometimes after a long, hard day they were the only thing that made sense."

"I still do that. Sit on my wooden step, shut my eyes and just breathe. It puts things into perspective when I think my life is getting too hard, or that I'm just not good enough. And when I'm sitting there, sometimes I can almost feel you sitting there with me. Going through the same struggles, thinking the same thoughts, trying to put things into perspective."

She leaned her head against his chest and listened to the steady rhythm of his heart. Everything about Arlo was steady. She'd always loved that about him, especially as nothing in her life ever seemed steady. "I don't have a balcony now, and my front steps—I live in a brownstone and they open straight onto the sidewalk." And she didn't have him there with her. That, more than anything else, made the difference.

"Does it have a real front door?" he asked.

"It does, with a proper lock."

"I could be jealous, you know."

She leaned her head back and looked up at his face—his beautiful face. His eyes. His curls. His neck. All with so many memories... "I could send you a proper door when I get home."

"Or give me a proper kiss now," he replied.

Her breath caught in her throat as he took her mouth, the stubble of his beard rough on her skin. But she liked the rugged look of it, the intense feel of it against her, primitive and wild. More sensual and appealing than the clean-shaven face she'd kissed all those years ago.

She wanted to resist him now, knew she should, but nothing in her would acquiesce to that insane notion, and a faint moan recklessly escaping her lips affirmed how very little she could, or would, resist. And all it took was that whisper of a moan to ignite Arlo, causing him to press hard into her, hold her harder, kiss her harder.

Layla's knees went weak with her desire for more of him, and as his mouth roamed without discretion, leaving a trail of heat against the soft curve of her throat then the delicate flesh of her ear, he was the one who groaned, but loud and guttural. For the stars in the heavens to hear.

Layla's arm, where it pressed against Arlo's, burned. But with her free arm she reached up and ran her fingers through his hair, through the curls she'd loved so dearly for so long. Then stood on tiptoe to kiss his neck. Baby-soft kisses, the ones that always gave him goosebumps. That ones that did so even now. "What do we do about this?" she asked, her voice so overcome with want and need it was barely audible. Dear heaven, she wanted the man she'd always wanted, and didn't know how to have.

CHAPTER EIGHT

THE HOTEL ROOM was hot and stuffy, and basic by any definition of the word. But by the time they'd secured the room for the night none of that had mattered. In fact, it hadn't been until just now that Layla had seen the lizard on the wall opposite the bed. Make that lizards—plural. Three of them, simply hanging there and watching.

"They're staring at us," she said to Arlo.

He was sprawled in bed next to her, the bedsheet coming up only to his waist. She, on the other hand, had her part of it pulled up to just below her chin.

"They're just small house geckos," he explained. "*Jing jok*, as they're called here. Harmless. Oh, and they're supposed to bring good luck. So we have three times the luck going for us."

She looked at their clothes piled in a heap on the floor. And two empty bottles of wine on the dresser. They'd stopped for another on their way to the hotel. Regrets? Not at all. In fact, she would have been contented to stay there all day, lounging, making love, spending the day the way they'd occasionally done when they'd both managed to have the same day off with nothing to do.

"Breakfast in bed would be nice," she said, looking at the chip and candy wrappers wadded and tossed at the trash can, but not into it, littering the floor.

"Actually, that would be brunch. And I could go down to the vending machines and grab us more junk food, since this place doesn't have a restaurant."

She shook her head. "I think after the way we indulged last night..."

He chuckled. "We sure did. Three times, if I remember correctly. But all that wine is kind of blurring my thoughts."

She scooted over next to him and laid her head on his bare chest. "I've never been in a hotel like this before." She looked across at the walls. Cement blocks painted yellow. And the furniture—one bed, one rickety chair and a dresser. "Is this where you bring all your women?" she asked, twining her fingers in his soft mat of chest hair.

"What? You're not impressed?"

"I saw the sign informing us we have to pay extra to use the shower."

"But it's in the room. That's better than many of the budget hotels offer. And the room came with a sheet, no extra cost." Arlo rolled slightly to his side and pulled her into his arms. "Unfortunately, all good things must come to an end. We've got a hospital to attend, and the nurse who went down to stay there for us has to leave later this afternoon."

"How did he manage to show up at just the right time?"

"Sylvie called him when she knew we probably wouldn't make it back for quite a while. She was actually in the village, having a pastry from Dusit's stall, when she saw what was happening, so it worked out well for us."

"I was dreading the ride back so late last night. After everything that went on…" She shook her head. "I suppose as good doctors we should check in on Virote before we leave."

"As good doctors I suppose we should conserve water when we shower."

"Hope it's warm," she said.

"Anything's better than a dribbling hose sticking through a window. And it does have a stopcock, so the dribble isn't continuous."

Layla laughed. "You know what? Even the

thought of that shower doesn't ruin my mood. After last night..."

"What about last night?" he asked, tucking his index finger under the edge of the sheet and starting to edge it down from her neck. "And do you suppose we should, um, get our money's worth out of this luxurious room before we leave?"

"Depends," she said, sliding down slightly in the bed, then yanking the sheet entirely off him, exposing every bare inch of the most glorious body she'd ever known.

"On what?"

"On if you can put blindfolds on those geckos. Good luck or not, I don't want them watching what I'm about to do."

"Sounds interesting." He rolled totally to his side and propped up his head on his hand. "So, tell me, what would that be?"

She smiled, wrinkling her nose, tossing away the sheet altogether, then also turning on her side to face him. "Let's just say it'll be well worth the effort of blindfolding the geckos."

"Blindfold them, hell. They're going out to the garden."

"Then be glad we rented a room *with* a window, because I'd hate to see you parading down the hall in nothing but a sheet, carrying three geckos." She looked down and grinned. "Especially in *that* condition. On second thought, I think the geckos can wait."

His preference would have been cuddling up with Layla for the rest of the day. It was nice, getting away. Nice not having to worry about so many things. Nice simply feeling human again. No expectations of him. No patients running after him. No nothing. And while he did love his hospital, getting away from it occasionally was necessary.

Unfortunately, that rarely happened. Not because he couldn't get medical coverage for a day or two. He could. But there was nothing that motivated him to go off somewhere alone. And that's where he'd been most of his time here. Somewhere alone. Come to think of it, it had been a long time since he'd shared a bed with anybody for anything other than a few quick moments.

The last person, in fact the only person he'd ever spent an entire night with, was Layla. And that had been so long ago, and they had been in such dire straits by that time, most of the memory was a blur. But he had a new memory or two now. And as he pulled the SUV off to the side of the road, just under the giant fig tree, he laid his head back against the seat, closed his eyes and sighed.

"Something wrong?"

"Just trying to hold on a little longer. Right now, we're still lovers, basking in an afterglow. When I go past the fig tree, we're doctors who will be facing a dozen or more people who missed us when we were gone. I'm just not quite ready to pass the fig tree yet."

"You do know that we're probably going to be up working all night, don't you?"

"You do know that I don't have to care until I'm on the other side of the fig tree, don't you?" He reached over and took hold of her hand. "It was good, Layla. And I'm not just talking about the sex. It was good just being with you, talking, doing nothing, doing everything. Sort of like old times, the way we used to do."

"But you know we're not those two people anymore."

"Life really got in the way, didn't it?"

"I think it does for most people. When you're younger you hope you can capture a single, perfect moment and spend the rest of your life in it. Then add some age, and experience, and you realize that perfect moments are just that—perfect moments. You can't capture them, and you certainly can't spend the rest of your life inside them because reality does finally rear up and show its ugly or even not-so-ugly face."

"And a fig tree is just a fig tree, no matter

which side of it you're sitting on. Anyway, I promised a house call sometime later today or this evening," he said, starting the engine again. "And I need to check some stitches I put in one of the children a couple of days ago. And one of us has to go give another pep talk to Dusit..."

What was the point of even thinking about anything personal between them could ever be more than what they'd just had? That one perfect moment or, in their case, night. She had a mission and she wasn't going to stop until she'd completed it. And he was only the means to her carrying out her mission.

He knew that, but it didn't take away the feelings for Layla that were growing. And they were growing fast, which was a huge problem. Because what he was thinking about was something he couldn't have. Just like last time. And what he had was something Layla wouldn't deal with for more than her allotted two months. So, where did that leave them? On a bumpy road back to the village. That's where.

"You awake?" Layla poked her head into the hut, only to find Arlo stretched out on his mat. They'd spent all of last evening and the whole day today chasing down minor complaints, he going one way through the village and she another.

"Pensri Buajan will be by in a while with food. Apparently, several of the women got together and cooked for us again—actually, they cooked for the whole village, in celebration of saving Virote's life. So we're to be the guests of honor at another celebration." She raised her foot and nudged him in the shoulder, only to have him turn on his side, away from her. "You don't get to sleep through it, Arlo. A lot of people have gone to the trouble of doing this for us, and the least you can do is show up."

"Bad bedside manner, Doctor," he mumbled. "You're never supposed to kick your patient under any circumstances."

"First, you're not my patient. Second, I didn't kick. I nudged."

"Nudge me again like that, and I'll take you to the floor."

Layla laughed. "You're such a faker, Arlo. Being mean-spirited doesn't suit you. You can't even pretend to do a good job of it." For effect, she nudged him with her foot again, only this time he was too quick for her, rolling over before her foot contacted his shoulder, then grabbing it and holding it.

"Put me down," she warned him, balancing herself on one foot. "Or else—"

"Or else what?" He grinned mischievously. "Tell me, Layla. What will you do?"

"This," she said, trying to twist away from him. Only she lost her balance and ended up on top of him.

"Didn't work," he teased, holding onto her as she tried to struggle free. Truth was, he liked her there. Didn't want to let her go.

"I've been pinned down by worse than you, Arlo Benedict."

"Who pinned you?" he asked, his face dangerously close to her.

"His name was James, big brute of a five-year-old. Launched off the exam table and grabbed me around the neck. But I made fast work of that. Took care of him in the blink of an eye."

"How?"

"Bribery. Two lollipops. He was a sucker for a couple of suckers."

"Do you have two lollipops for me?" he asked, still holding on but now more like rubbing her back than latching onto her.

"You had your lollipops yesterday, and the day before. Sort of like paying in advance." She twisted a bit, only managing to find herself deeper in his embrace rather than being free of him.

"And what if I want another one right now?"

"We don't have a door, and I'm not an exhibitionist. I don't like giving you lollipops where everybody can watch us. And because the meal is coming to us—actually, to the hospital—since it's large enough to hold more people than this place is, I think anything we might do would definitely be on exhibition."

"Why do you always have to make so much sense?" he protested, rolling over to his back then sitting up.

"Someone has to." She headed toward the door, then turned back to him. "I'm glad I came here, Arlo. And that's not just about the promotion. It's nice that we're reconnecting, again. I've missed that. And you. I've missed you."

This wasn't what he wanted or needed to hear. He was already soft in the head over this thing, and now with Layla going soft— No, it's not what he needed because, like the first time, they both knew where this would end. Which made everything they were doing a game. They were simply playing games. "Look, I've got to go check on Achara now that she's home again. I'll be back for the party in a while." With that, he pushed himself off the floor, grabbed his medical bag and was on his scooter, putt-putting his way down the road before Layla could say or do something to change his mind. He didn't want to change his mind. This wasn't going to work, and the games were going to stop. Otherwise the rest of her time here was going to stretch out into a miserable eternity he didn't want. Not at all.

The party was long over, and Arlo had never returned. She understood why, and she also understood that her feelings and his were the same. They were going round and round, fighting something they couldn't fight. And it wasn't for the first time. This time they were experienced at it. Knew exactly what it was and where it was going.

And with the better part of two months still stretching out ahead of them—this was a mistake. She'd known, when she'd volunteered for this duty, how it might work out. But there hadn't been a day in the past five years that bits and pieces of Arlo hadn't been in her thoughts. He had always been there in some way. In a surgery she'd known Arlo was particularly skilled at doing, in the twinkle in Ollie's eyes—the one Arlo had inherited from him—in his favorite pillow that she'd tucked back on a closet shelf and couldn't bear to get rid of after he'd left her.

She didn't know if she had it in her to go back to that place. It had been so bad then, and now that she understood him even better—she didn't even want to think about it. So, on her way from the hospital to the hut to which she'd been summoned, she tried putting everything out of her thoughts by counting steps. Eyes to the dirt road, counting out loud.

"Well, you aren't what I was expecting." The man, her patient, was older, rugged and very handsome, with silver hair and a short beard with thin, neatly trimmed sides. Silver, like his hair. He was sitting up in the first bed of an otherwise empty hut. Looking flushed, breathing hard. But smiling. And he was not a native.

"Who were you expecting?"

"Well, specifically, Arlo. But you're a pleasant surprise. It's been a good, long while since I've seen a doctor, and seeing how you're a lady doc, more's the better."

He was charming. That much was certain. "Well, Arlo's— Actually, I'm not sure where he is. Probably on a house call somewhere. I'm Layla. Layla Morrison." She held out her hand to shake his. "And I'm assuming you're one of the Dr. Benedicts. Since you're not Arlo, and not Ollie, then you must be—"

"Ward. Does the family resemblance show that much?"

"Trust me, I've been around various Benedict doctors long enough that I can spot them a mile away. So, what's the complaint?"

"A bit of a snakebite, I'm sorry to say. Just above my right boot."

"Arlo wears sandals," she said, as she rolled

up Ward's cargo pants to find that the bite mark was above the top of his boot. And also a cross cut mark, where he'd probably tried sucking out the venom himself.

"I've warned him about that, but he never seems to think his need is greater than someone else's. Last time he had boot money, he spent it on some wood and nails to build a ramp for one of the older women here. She was having difficulty getting up her steps. Time before that, I think it was to help someone start a sugarcane crop. That's what my son does. Puts almost everyone ahead of himself. But you know that, don't you?"

"He's told you about me?"

"Not in so many words. But because he chooses his few words about you carefully, I think you're the one who impacted his life in ways I'd always hoped someone would."

"In ways that wouldn't let us be together. Not in the sense you and your wife were."

"He always said you were ambitious, but ambitions are an odd thing, Layla. Everybody has them, of course. But they can change, and they can certainly be what you want to make of them. Arlo is just as ambitious as you are, and his ambitions are no less important than yours. He told me it was your ambitions that broke you up the first time. But it was about his ambitions as well. He just couldn't see that at the time. I doubt any of us can when we're as involved as the two of you were. And just keep in mind, ambitions are not objective. In fact, they're quite the opposite. Subjective as hell. And that's the end of my fatherly lecture. So, tell me, the bite…" He smiled, even though his face was beginning to bead with sweat. "Bugger was a red-necked keelback. They're usually not aggressive, but I must have done something to make this one angry because it came at me before I had a chance to step away. Went right up to the top of my boot."

"So, since I don't know my snakes, you tell me: Are we in trouble here?"

"Somewhat," Ward admitted.

"How long did this snake have hold of you? Was it less than one second? One to three seconds? Three to five? Ten? Sixty?"

"Probably thirty to forty. It wouldn't let go."

"Which means it had a lot of time to squeeze plenty of venom into your leg. And judging by the second set of marks, it bit you again."

"Well, that little—"

"I don't think getting yourself upset, causing your blood pressure to increase, is going to help you."

"A bottle of whiskey would, though. If you happen to have one handy. Which you probably don't since Arlo prefers wine. Something that came about in his time with you, I believe?"

"Well, now I know I had some kind of good influence on him."

"You had your influence, Layla. Probably more than you know, or more than he'd ever tell you. Anyway, while I've treated snakebites before, this is my first time to be bitten, and as a patient I'm beginning to have some worries over the outcome of this thing. Especially now that a headache and nausea are setting in."

"Well, we have a good stock of antivenin..."

"Not this, you don't. Which may turn this into a sticky situation shortly."

"Are you sure?"

"I know my snakes, and I especially know my antivenins. You don't live most of your seventy years here and not know what's crawling in the grass, and what's available to counteract its poison."

Now she was beginning to panic. Her patient was telling her about his prospects, not the other way around. And she didn't like what she was hearing. There had to be a way—Arlo would know. He always knew. "I think I'm going to go find Arlo and see what he has to say," she said, trying not to sound as alarmed as she was feeling.

"He'll say the same thing I said. We're in trouble here."

She gave the man's arm a squeeze. "If I can do a field amputation hanging upside down in a tree, this little snakebite should be a breeze." Not that it was, or that she even believed her own words. "I'll be right back." She saw the woman who owned the hut, Naak, standing in the shadows, watching, then pointed to a chair across from Ward. "Can you ask her to stay with you?" Layla asked Ward.

He chuckled weakly. "And to think I only came to let Arlo be the first to know I'm getting married again. Now I'm not so sure."

"Married?"

"If I survive this." He lay back on the bed and shut his eyes. "Don't worry. I'm not going to die in the next few minutes. I just proposed to her a couple of weeks ago and she'll kill me if I die before we marry." He chuckled weakly, then dropped off to sleep.

Layla ran so hard and fast through the village, stopping to inquire after Arlo every few seconds, she didn't even remember arriving at Dusit's home, which was where she was directed. But there she was, standing outside, trying to catch her breath so she could talk to Arlo.

"Layla?" he asked, stepping out, still holding the blood sugar monitor.

"It's your dad," she panted. "Snakebite. Red-necked something-back."

"Damn," he muttered, jamming the monitor into his pocket then dashing back inside to grab his bag. "How long ago?" he asked, running back outside and not even slowing when he passed her.

She ran to catch up with him. "Maybe twenty minutes."

"Any symptoms showing yet?"

"A few. Nausea, headache, sweating. Exhaustion. Arlo, he said we don't have the antivenin."

"Nobody does. It's manufactured in Japan and it's in short supply because a red-necked keelback doesn't usually bite. I've never had that antivenin because I've never had a patient bitten by one of those." He stopped at the entrance to Naak's hut, then shut his eyes. "They're so docile children play with them."

She stepped up to his side. "Well, this one wasn't playing. He bit your dad twice and the envenomation took a long time. I think he's pumped full of the poison. I didn't ask him, but he said it was fatal. Is it?"

Rather than answering, Arlo looked down at Layla. "He might not have enough time left for us to get him what he needs. It's only made in

Japan, and you have to have quite a pull with the pharmaceutical company to get it. I'm thinking since Eric lives in Japan, he might have that pull." He sucked in his breath then headed up the stairs. "Go out as far as you can until you get a signal. Then call him. It's a long shot. But it's all we have." He tossed her his phone with Eric's number in it.

"Arlo, your dad tried sucking out his own venom."

"Hopefully, that will prolong his life." Those were his last words before entering the hospital. And seconds later Layla was on her way to find a mobile signal. Wondering what anybody in circumstances like this would do if not for Arlo—and her. For the first time she felt connected. Maybe more connected than she ever had before. She mattered in this. She needed to be here. And it wasn't she who needed the support. It was everybody out here. Everybody. And Arlo. Especially Arlo.

CHAPTER NINE

"HOW'S THE SNAKEBITE VICTIM?" Arlo asked, as he entered the clinic, fighting to remain calm when nothing inside him was.

"He's seen better days," Ward admitted, as Arlo reached his bedside and bent down to give his old man a hug.

"So, how did you get into this mess, Dad?"

"Wasn't paying attention. Thinking happy thoughts, I suppose."

He peeled back the sheet and looked at his dad's leg. It wasn't necrotic yet, but it wasn't good. There was too much swelling, his dad was diaphoretic and having some trouble breathing. "Tell me, what were those happy thoughts?" he asked, as he hooked up an oxygen mask to the cannister he'd grabbed on his way over. "Anything I should know about before I put this thing on you and tell you not to talk?"

"Well, if I do come out of this somehow, I'm getting married."

Arlo blinked hard at the news. "Seriously? Who? How'd you meet her?"

"She's a nurse who works in the tourist clinic with me near Angkor Wat. I've been working around there quite a while now and— What can I say? She's a great lady and I'm not dead yet—well, that remains to be seen, I suppose."

"This isn't going to kill you, Dad. Maybe make you suffer a bit, but..." He faked a smile as he pulled out a bottle of antiseptic to clean the wound. "Does she make you happy?" he asked, uncapping the bottle and pouring it over his dad's leg.

"Does Layla make you happy?"

"Ah, the question that has no answer." He placed the mask on his dad's face and tightened the elastic straps for a tight fit.

"It has an answer, son. I saw it in her face as clearly as I see it in yours." He reached up to wipe the sweat from his face, but his hands were too shaky. "So, what's the plan here, son? Because if I were the doc in charge, I would be preparing the patient for the inevitable."

"But you're not the doc here, and the plan is Layla getting through to Eric who will ride in on his white horse all the way from Japan with the antivenin." Such a long shot, but it was the only one he had unless someone, someplace else, had some antivenin. Which didn't seem likely given its scarcity. "So, right now, you need to rest. The more active you are, the more the venom spreads."

"Isn't that something I taught you when you were, what? Seven or eight?" Finally, his eyes drooped shut and he took a deep breath that indicated sleep was already overtaking him.

"I was eight, Dad," Arlo said, slapping at the tears streaking down his cheeks. "What you taught me when I was seven was how important the work here is." He took hold of his dad's hand and stayed there, sitting on the edge of the bed, until Layla finally came back almost two hours later. The first thing she did was rush to the bed, look down and sigh a sigh of relief when she discovered that Ward was only sleeping. The second thing she did was pull Arlo into her arms and simply hold him. "We're going to get through this," she whispered. "I promise. We're going to get through this."

He heard the words but had no response to them. All he knew was that he was grateful Layla was the one with him now, whichever way this went. He needed her. Only her.

"Eric's going to grab a supply of the antivenin and fly down here. It's going to be a long flight, Arlo. But he's on his way."

"It may be too late," he said, not even trying to hide the discouragement in his voice.

"How long…?" She didn't finish her question. How could she when what she wanted to know was how long Ward had to live? She didn't know and didn't want to ask. But she had to take charge here and leave Arlo time to simply be his father's son.

"Ten to twelve hours. Maybe up to a day, depending on my dad's sensitivity level."

"Then Eric will get here in time."

"Or it may take only an hour, then all of this is for nothing."

"Not for nothing, Arlo," she said, sitting in a chair opposite him, her hand on his knee while he still held his dad's hand. "For your dad. Or for any patient in the same situation. You don't quit. You never have. And you won't now."

"It's so hard doing this alone. Doing the things I must do. Facing the things I must face. With my parents, they had each other to help them through. I have a civet cat, which says a lot, doesn't it?"

Villagers were beginning to assemble outside, all of them knowing now that the patient was Doc Arlo's dad. People were bringing food. Various drinks. Women were offering to clean the hospital. Several men were across the street, repairing Arlo's leaking roof. It was an amazing sight, watching everybody come together the way they were. And not just because Arlo was their doctor. They loved him. He was part of them. Part of the heart and soul of everybody here. "Just look at them," she said, as they were going into their third hour of waiting. "You're not alone here, Arlo. Even Dusit is out there, toting a basket of sweets for you."

He chuckled. "Of course, he would. Which means he's going to need another test shortly, and probably a shot."

"You take wonderful care of these people. In turn, they take wonderful care of you. And if you ask me, that's an almost perfect way to run your medical practice, minus the hardships, of course." She stood, then crossed over to the bed to check Ward's vital signs. Currently, he wasn't losing ground, and that's the best they could hope for. "I could sit here, if you want to go grab some sleep."

"I can't sleep," he said, standing, then stretching.

She heard his neck pop. "Can I fix that for you?" she asked, pointing him to her chair rather than the side of the bed.

He didn't answer, but he did sit where she wanted him to, and positioned himself for the neck massage. And the instant she applied pressure with her fingers, he moaned. "Best hands

I've ever experienced," he said, relaxing into her touch. "You always knew when I needed it, too, didn't you?"

"We might have been bad at some things, but I never ignored you, Arlo. In fact, there were nights I'd lie awake in bed simply to watch you sleep."

"I knew that."

"Seriously?"

"Seriously. And I liked knowing you were doing it, even though most of the time you weren't sleeping. So, tell me. Why did you watch?"

"I loved the way that your hair would curl down over your forehead. And your neck—did I ever tell you that you have the sexiest neck I've ever seen on anybody? After you'd gone to sleep I loved nuzzling into your neck. Or were you even asleep?"

"Nope," he said, finally fully relaxing. "Not all the time anyway. And I did enjoy the way you'd sort of sneak into me and position yourself so I could feel you pressed to my neck. Sometimes you'd kiss me there. Just a light one. Trying not to wake me up, I suppose."

"So, whatever happened to *that* couple?"

"One went to Thailand, and one didn't. That's the way we started our relationship, and the way we finished it. We both knew what would happen from the beginning, but I think we—or, at least, I—got sidetracked somewhere along the way.

"Did you ever think I might stay with you, Layla?"

"Not think as much as hope."

"But you never asked. Never said a word about it."

"Because we couldn't get past it, Arlo. Not then. And I didn't want to keep on hurting over it so no, I never asked, because I didn't want to be rejected. Especially by the only man I'd ever loved."

"Was I?" he asked.

"You still are. Nothing about that has ever changed." Layla sniffed back tears as she moved her massage more toward the side of his neck. "But nothing about us has ever changed either, has it?"

"You said you loved me before but went right past it, so I didn't know. And this is the first time I really believe that you did…maybe still do. But never when we were together."

"What I couldn't say wasn't what I felt. And I was so afraid of what I felt because the people in my life didn't love me the way I thought they should. I saw my friends get that kind of love. Even just now I saw it between you and your dad. But what I got was always…compromised.

There was always another component to it. Another agenda. So I suppose you could say that for me the non-resolution was safer than what I feared the resolution might be."

"Which was why you were so distant so much of the time."

"I was afraid to get closer, Arlo. Because I knew the ending to our story from the very first page."

In the bed, Ward stirred and opened his eyes. Arlo jumped up to be at his side, and Ward gave him a very weak thumbs-up. "Everything's in motion, Dad. Now we're just waiting for the antivenin to arrive. Eric's bringing it, by the way."

Ward attempted a nod and a smile, then went back to sleep.

"So, what is it between you and your brother that you're not close? His money? Do you resent it the way you resented mine?"

"I didn't resent your money, Layla. Money's never been a big thing in my life one way or the other. But when we were together you used your money as a crutch, shutting me out of places where I really belonged. When you had a problem, rather than letting me help you through it, you went on a shopping spree. When you had your infrequent contact with your parents and ended up all depressed, and I'd try to be understanding, you'd push me away and—"

"Go on a shopping spree. It was easier than dealing with the emotions. And it's what I learned growing up. When I had a problem, rather than my parents trying to help me through it, they bought me things. *See this pearl necklace, darling? It'll make you feel better.* When you hear that enough, you start believing it. But what about Eric? If it wasn't about money, then what?"

"We just haven't had our opportunity yet. There was resentment in the past because we shared a mother I knew and he didn't, but we're over that. Or almost over. And as far as his money—or even yours—goes, I don't resent it, but I don't want my life to be about it either."

"And you think mine is?"

"It was. You were the one who supported me, Layla. Took pity on the poor resident, invited him to live with you. Paid for the expensive meals out when you wanted to go out and I was good eating a bowl of cereal at home. You were the one who bought me a watch that cost more than I'd make in two or three years, because you thought it would look good on my arm. And Eric—shortly after he was married, and finally happy, he wanted to come in like a storm trooper and turn my hospital into something that would never work here. For me, when money entered the picture, I got pushed aside. Or what I wanted got pushed aside."

"And what you want is…?"

"What I have. I've never been like other people, Layla. I'm simple. Not in the head, but in the way I want to spend my life. People get too complicated, too cluttered and they lose themselves in all that. Eric did. He was drowning when Michi, his wife, saved him. And you—the kind of ambitions you have—that's way over my head. I'd much rather hike five miles into the jungle to treat a throat infection than sit behind a desk and only come out when protocol dictates I do.

"But people assume that because I'm poor, and will likely spend my life that way, that I'm to be pitied. So they buy me expensive watches and send architects to a jungle to design a state-of-the-art mini-medical center. While their—*your*—intentions may be good, they're not my intentions. But that gets overlooked."

"Wow," she said, stunned. "Have I ever done anything right?"

"You haven't done anything wrong. Neither has Eric. People who care for each other want the best. Only in my case, my best wasn't good enough for the people who cared for me." He glanced at the clock on the wall, then at his dad. "It's getting close," he said, as Ward was beginning to turn a peculiar shade of gray. Layla had put an IV in him hours ago, and the oxygen was helping his breathing a little bit. But he was burning with fever now and shaking so hard the vibration of it traveled through the bed and down to the wooden floor.

"I'll bet Eric will be here within two hours."

"If he holds on that long."

She could feel Arlo's despair. Even though he was fighting hard not to show the fear, she saw it. The distant look in his eyes. The impatient way he ran his hand through his hair. Shifting positions sometimes several times a minute. No looking directly at his dad unless it was in some medical way. "He's in good physical condition overall, Arlo. That's to his benefit."

"Pep talks don't work here," he said, bolting off the bed. "So please—" He stopped, shook his head. "I need some air. Won't be gone long." With that, he strode out the hospital door, pushed his way through all the people out there and headed for a path straight into the jungle. Layla watched him from the window but didn't go after him. He needed to be alone. With his dad being so sick, and with all the talking they'd been doing, she knew that as well as she knew her own name. Arlo needed space and she wouldn't deprive him of it.

* * *

"It's complicated, isn't it?" Sylvie said. She'd come to help and now she was bringing a cup of tea to Layla, who was sitting bedside with Ward, holding his hand. "It turns your world around and there's nothing you can do about it except let it happen and hope you don't perish in it somewhere."

"I didn't mean to fall in love with him the first time I did, and I certainly didn't mean to do it again. And you're right. It's complicated."

"If you want it to be. When I was married, we didn't allow complications. My husband was much older than I and I knew our time together wouldn't be as long as I wanted. So, every day was a gift. And I'm not saying we didn't have problems. Every couple does. But we didn't let them come between us. Which is what I believe is happening to you and Arlo. You're letting the complications keep you apart."

"But how can you get through them?"

"You let the love in. Freely. Fully. Once it's there you'll find that the complications aren't so…complicated."

"So why did you stay here after your husband died? Didn't it hurt to do that?"

"It did, but we loved it here. And that's the thing I can't bear to walk away from. It's still here, and it still keeps me connected to the love of my life." She smiled fondly. "This is my home now. I can't leave it. As they say, home is where the heart is."

And her heart and home were with Arlo. Which proved Sylvie right. Suddenly her complications weren't as complicated as she knew what she had to do. Finally, after all this time, she knew. Now she only hoped it would be the same for Arlo.

Arriving in the nick of time was just that. Eric had arrived in the nick of time with the antivenin. And now Arlo was watching his brother load his dad onto a helicopter for transport to one of the best hospitals in Bangkok. He'd promised to come back tomorrow to give Arlo a lift there to be with his dad.

And Layla—she was working hard and fast to take all their medical calls. Insulin shots, maternity checks, rashes, everything.

He caught up with her outside Dusit's vendor stall and literally had to take hold of her arm to keep her in place for a moment. "He's going to be OK," he said to her.

She smiled. "That's what the talk on the street is all about."

"Except you don't understand the talk on the street."

"I have my ways, Arlo."

"Like I didn't know that before. So, care to come sit with me for a little while?"

"Will it involve a cup of tea?"

"And a pair of arms around you, if you'd like that."

"Ah, the one offer I can't refuse." She slipped her hand into his. "Are you OK? You look exhausted."

"Probably because I am exhausted. But I'm too wound up to sleep."

"Then think nice, warm soak in a tub."

"I would, except for two things. No warm water. No tub."

She smiled. "That's what you think, Dr. Benedict." She pointed down the road to several men who were hefting an old, galvanized tub of some sort into their hut. "Problem one, solved."

"It's for the water buffalo to drink out of," he said, more frustrated than amused. "Not for people to soak in."

"It can be anything you want it to be, Arlo."

"Then what becomes of the poor water buffalo who's thirsty?" He knew she meant well, but all he wanted to do was talk about their problems rather than try to solve them in some poor water buffalo's trough. Maybe this was a bad idea. Maybe he wasn't ready. Obviously, she wasn't. And right now he simply didn't have it in him to work it out because this was the old Layla, trying to fix matters with her materialist outlook. Expensive watches, a water trough. It was all the same. Something meant to push away the reality of what they needed to talk about.

"Look, let's talk later, OK? Without the trough. Maybe when we can take our situation more seriously." Bad words. He knew that from the look on her face. But it was too late to take them back, and he really didn't want to try and explain. Not now. Maybe not ever since they'd had a variation on this theme before and nothing good had come out of it. "When I'm up to it?"

"Up to it, Arlo? Or do you mean up to dealing with me?"

He held his arms up in surrender. "Look, now's not the time. We might say things we'd regret later on, and I don't want to do that. Not again." And another bad turn of the word. He was sinking here, and didn't know how to save himself. So, for now, he wasn't even going to try. And hopefully, after he'd rested, when they'd come back around to this, and they would, he'd make better sense of it. He wanted to. But in his current condition he wasn't optimistic.

"Just as well," she said, pulling her hand from his. "I have several more patients to see, plus several hours of charting ahead of me. Need to write up a progress report for Ollie, too. Think I'll take it over to Sylvie's tomorrow, scan it and send it to him right away."

Yep, the same old Layla. Different circumstances, different conditions, same old Layla. And here he was hoping—well, it didn't matter what he hoped, did it? They really hadn't come so very far from where they'd left off last time. One of them wanting to talk, the other putting it off. The beginning of the end of something they both wanted but didn't know how to hold onto.

"Looks like the lady isn't happy with you," Eric said, coming up behind Arlo. "I think she's giving you the cold shoulder." It was early morning, the day after Ward had gone to Bangkok, and Eric was there to fetch his brother.

"To be honest, I'm used to it. That's our history because Layla is ambitious in ways I'm not and, in the end, that's what causes our problems. I can't win over her ambitions and she doesn't see why I can't put aside what I want so she can have what she wants. That's what killed us the first time, and what will kill us again. We can't be together and still go our separate ways which is why I think she is going to have to go back early. This isn't doing either of us any good. We can talk and talk until there are no words left, but there's no resolution. Our destinies are different."

"And you can't compromise?"

"How?" Arlo shook his head. "Look, I know that you're happy now and you want everybody to be as happy as you are. But life doesn't always work out that way."

"I gave up a billion-dollar corporation and moved halfway around the world because I loved Michi more than anything else in my life, and I would have moved heaven and earth to be with her. It was a small sacrifice considering all I've gotten in return. So maybe you just don't love Layla enough. Anyway, we need to fly. I stopped by to see your dad before I came back here and he's up and ready to get out of there. I think we need to fly to Bangkok, grab him, and we can come back. Maybe by that time I'll be able to meet her properly. Or, at the very least, she'll have forgiven you for being so dense about the ways of true love."

"Does it matter? This is history repeating itself."

"It does matter if you're going to patch things up and finally marry her."

"Who said anything about marriage?"

"I did, if you're smart."

"Do you really think I could adjust to living

a civilized life? Go back to New York and start to wear real shoes?"

"If Layla means that much to you, you can do anything."

Arlo looked up and down the main road of the village, somewhat pensively at first. Then he smiled. "I do have a brother who owns a fleet of airplanes, so getting back here from time to time wouldn't be a big deal, would it?"

"Any time you want to fly, it's there, waiting for you."

"You do realize that I'm about to become a man of material means, don't you?"

"Then I take it your destiny is in New York?"

"Working for my very ambitious wife, it seems."

Eric chuckled. "Welcome to the road that will lead you to be the happiest man in the world, next to me, of course. Now, on the way to Bangkok, let's discuss how we're going to manage the holidays. Your and Layla's place, or Michi's and mine?"

She wasn't sure what'd she heard, and when she'd realized she was practically eavesdropping, she walked away. But it sounded like Arlo was getting ready to send her away. Had she heard him saying they were about to go their separate ways?

Angry tears streamed down her face and she didn't even bother to blot them. She'd come to tell him she wanted to stay, wanted to find her happiness in the life that made him so happy. But he had other ideas, and he didn't even have the decency to discuss them with her.

Well, maybe she deserved that. Still, it hurt. Hurt worse this time because she knew so much more. Knew that she loved him and how valuable that love was. Knew she could make sacrifices to be with him. Knew that her true happiness was with Arlo and not in her ambitions and agendas. She'd watched him. Everything he did only made her love him more. And the respect he received—he couldn't walk away from that. She didn't want him to. She'd never had that from anyone. Didn't know what it felt like. But she was so proud of the respect Arlo had earned and, for the first time, knew that was enough for her.

But, in the end, maybe she simply was his holiday. The one he'd get together with every few years, then walk away from when, yet again, he realized their gap was too wide to bridge. Or she realized once more that sometimes love wasn't enough. Well, not now. Not while she had some dignity still intact. Not much, but some. And this time—there was closure.

She'd seen his world, even fancied herself

a part of it. Deluded herself into thinking she was fitting in. She was wrong, though. Wrong in so many ways. So she'd go. Go her separate way, like he'd told his brother they would do. But with her head held high, as she'd given it a chance. And failed. Only problem was, even while her head was being held high, her heart was breaking in a way it would never be put together again. Nobody compared to Arlo. She knew that even more now, this second time, than she had the first. Nobody compared, nobody ever would. And in a way, that sealed her destiny.

"It's nothing, Mrs. Anderson. Just a minor infection in your incision. I'll take a culture and call in a prescription. If it doesn't clear up in a week, make another appointment."

All day—consultations, scheduling surgeries, scheduling follow-ups. Not even many surgeries to perform as now her work was all about the administrative side of what she'd rather be doing. But in the jungle. She was assistant chief of surgery now, yet her duties made her restless. Meaning what she'd worked so hard to get wasn't what she wanted after all.

Arlo—she couldn't even begin to count the many times she'd thought of him this past month. Had shed tears. Gotten angry. Shed more tears. More than she'd counted on. More than she'd wanted. But she missed him in ways she'd never known one person could miss another. And working for his grandfather wasn't helping matters because Ollie was always the constant reminder of what she'd almost had.

But that wasn't going to last as she'd accepted the promotion on a temporary basis, then applied for a surgical position, no administration at all, in Texas. This time next week she'd be doing surgical repairs on cowboys.

"Could you pop the chart up on the screen for my next patient?" she asked Jackie Hastings, one of the clerks. "I can't get the computer to do anything, and according to the list I saw printed out earlier, I'm supposed to see somebody named Jeanne Kingston."

"She's on the list, Doctor. But there's another name before hers. It's classified as immediate care."

"By?"

"You," Jackie said. "That's your name on the schedule override."

"Except I didn't override the schedule." Maybe Ollie had, accidentally. Or one of the other three staff doctors. "Well, is the patient male or female?"

Jackie looked perplexed. "There's really no information here except a name I can't read and the diagnosis of heart problems. And it's scrawled on the admit sheet, not logged into the computer."

"So spell the name for me."

Jackie looked at the handwritten admission form and shook her head. "Fig—fig something. Figgy?" She squinted her eyes, then shook her head. "Sorry, I can't make sense of it. I think his name is Mr. Fig?" She squinted again. "Fig-tree. His name is Mr. Figtree."

Layla gasped, then dropped her note tablet on the desk. "Where is he? What room?"

"Seven," Jackie said. But by the time the word was totally out of her mouth, Layla was running down the hall toward Exam Seven.

"What are you doing here?" Layla choked, fighting hard to keep her composure as she ran into Mr. Figtree's room.

"I needed a doctor."

"For what you're describing as a heart problem."

"A very big heart problem," Arlo said, keeping a straight face.

"Then maybe I should refer you straight to a cardiologist." Dear lord, she wanted to throw herself into his arms. But she didn't know if she should, or if he'd even want it.

"Don't need one," he said.

"Why not?"

"Because I already know the cure."

"Which is?" she asked.

"A secret."

She stood there, scrutinizing him for a moment. He looked so good. But, then, Arlo always looked good. And she'd missed him so badly… "So the cure to your problem is a secret you're keeping from your doctor?"

"It might be. Or I might be ready to get cured." A smile began to curve his lips.

"How does that work?"

Please, please, please let this be what I hope it is.

"By divulging my secret to see what she can do about it."

"Is it a secret or a complication?"

He shrugged. "Remains to be seen. Why did you leave, Layla? You didn't even stay around long enough to say goodbye. When I got back from Bangkok, you were gone. Nothing left behind. And the medic who'd come to take over while I was gone had no idea why you left."

"I left because that's what you wanted me to do." But not what she'd wanted to do.

"I did, occasionally. I'll admit it. But if I'd known you'd actually do it, I would have stopped you."

"Why?"

"Because I love you. Because I want to spend

the rest of my life with you. Because I was so damned messed up that I didn't even realize I was pushing away the best thing I'd ever had in my life. I built my life around one thing, Layla, and you plowed through that so easily it scared me. Especially since I didn't want the same things out of life that you did."

"Things change, Arlo. I changed. But not until I realized that what I didn't want was what I wanted most. By then, though, it was too late. You were done with me."

"I wasn't done with you, Layla. I was done with me. At least, the part of me that wouldn't budge enough to let you in."

"Then why did you want me to leave?"

"I was coming with you, Layla. That's what changed. I was coming with you."

She shook her head. "How could you do that, Arlo? This isn't your life."

"Neither is Thailand, without you."

She shut her eyes, so afraid of what she expected to hear yet even more afraid that what she expected, and even wanted, wasn't going to happen. But this was the moment, wasn't it? That one moment when she'd either have everything she wanted or nothing at all. The one where, instead of running away from something, she had to run toward something. The one where she would have everything in her heart rather than trying to save her heart from the pain she always expected.

Arlo crossed over to her and pulled her into his arms. "You know this is where you belong, don't you?"

"I think I've always known that, even though I wouldn't admit it."

"There were two of us in that, Layla. Not just you alone. And suddenly it's not so easy. I've been rehearsing this since the day you left. Wanted to make sure I'd get it right before I came after you. Thought I'd finally got myself to the place where I could go through with it. But what I'm going to say scares me because it can change so many things—for both of us."

"With the way you live, I'd have thought change would be the least of your worries."

"The least, yet the biggest. That day you left… I was angry at first. Then resigned. Then hurt. I went through just about every emotion you can think of, trying to figure what I needed to do to make it right. Or if I should just let it go. Before I'd gone to Bangkok to get my dad, I'd decided to come back and tell you that I would come back here with you, love you, support you and do whatever it would take to make you happy because you were more important than anything else in my life. Like I told you, everybody always had other plans for me, and

I think some of what I was doing was simply to prove that I didn't need to be the object of anybody's pity.

"Where I was—I was poor. You knew that. And that was never going to change. Yet there you were, giving me gifts that cost a fortune, which only pointed out even more vividly just how poor I was. That, in turn, kept me from getting truly involved with you because I was afraid I'd always be seen as the one who wasn't capable of making it on my own. That I'd always need a handout.

"Yet here were these people who looked up to me. They didn't care that I didn't have proper boots or a decent vehicle. They cared for me the way I was. And it felt good, Layla. Damned good."

"I cared for you the way you were, Arlo."

"But always wanted to change me in subtle ways. And some not so subtle ways, too. The first time anyway. Then the second time I could still see it in you—all the questions you asked about why I was doing what I was doing. Every time you asked, it felt like I was letting you down by not being someone different. Yet the villagers loved me for who I am. It's quite a conflict, when you think about it."

"I never meant that," she said.

"I know. But sometimes it's hard to overcome your feelings, no matter how stupid they are."

"Or well founded. I know I gave you reason to think I believed you needed to change. Originally. I thought you did. But that was for my benefit, Arlo. Who you were and who I was—you were so far above me I knew that you'd catch onto it eventually. But if I could keep you tied to me in some way, it would work out. At least, that's what I thought."

"Why did you really come to Thailand?" he asked.

"It was my excuse to see you again. To see if anything was still there. But I also wanted that promotion—wanted it badly enough to work with a former lover under the worst of conditions."

"And?"

"That lasted until the first moment I saw you. Then everything changed, even though I didn't want to admit it."

"Yet you're admitting it now."

"I'm going to Texas next week, Arlo. Took a surgical position. No administration. Just surgery."

"Why?"

"I can't work here. My ambition here is what killed us. And working for Ollie, who's always a reminder…"

"Is your new hospital looking for another surgeon?"

"You'd hate it there. No civet cats."

"Speaking of which, he misses you. Actually, so did I, which is why I'm here. I love you, Layla Morrison. I have almost from the first moment I set eyes on you and I thought by forcing you to leave, I'd get myself back on track. But that track is you, and I want to spend the rest of my life with you, if you'll have me."

Besides her stomach churning, now her heart was beating faster. "I love you, too. For me, I think it was love always. The first time it just wasn't as mature or refined as it needed to be. And the second time, when I looked down and saw those hideous sandals and realized what kind of man practiced medicine in the jungle wearing the worst possible shoes, I knew it was real. I was…am proud of you for who you are, Arlo. For your sacrifices. For the way you've never compromised your beliefs.

"That's all I've ever been about—the compromises I had to make to get where I thought I wanted to be. Then, of all things, discovering it wasn't where I wanted to be at all. I was always scared, Arlo, that you'd get in my way. But what scared me even more was realizing you were my way, and that's exactly where I wanted to be. But I wasn't good enough."

"What do you mean, you're not good enough?"

"The way people respect you—I've never had that. Ollie respects my skills because they advance him, but he doesn't respect me. I know that, and I'm fine with it. And my parents—what they respect is nothing I could ever be about. They try their best, but it's not in them, and there's never been once when they've told me they were proud of me, or that I've done a good job. Then when I saw it, unspoken, between you and your dad..." She shook her head. "I don't fit into that, Arlo. I'm a good surgeon, but that's all I am. You, on the other hand, are so much more and I don't want you giving up everything you've done and earned to move to a place you'll hate, even if you do love me. That will destroy you bit by bit, and I couldn't live with myself knowing I'm the cause. You know where you need to be, and I've always envied that. Embrace it, Arlo. You're a lucky man to have it."

"I'd be a luckier man to have you. Sometimes we don't really know what we want until we've had it and lost it. I lost you once and I'm going to do that again. So, if it's here, fine. Or Texas, that's fine, too."

"Or a little village in Thailand?" she asked. "You'd do that?"

"When I bought my plane ticket to Texas,

I bought another one—to Thailand. I pinned them to my cork board and every time I walked by it, I thought about which one I'd use."

"And?"

"And I'd usually cry."

"Because?"

"Because the one I was most likely to use wasn't the one I wanted to use."

"Well, if you choose to use the one for Texas, I'll buy one, too. And I suppose I could get used to wearing a cowboy hat."

"And cover your beautiful hair? I won't have it. I love your hair. I don't want you covering it up for me."

"Then if not a cowboy hat, what?"

She reached up and ran her fingers through his hair. "I would have you, Arlo. In Thailand, where you belong. And where I want to belong."

"You can't mean that, Layla."

"Yes, I can. And I do. If you'll have me. But only in Thailand, Arlo. Only in our jungle village because where you're happy, that's where I'll be happy."

"And Texas?"

"No civet cats. And I really do need to be someplace with civet cats." She reached up, snaked her hands around his neck and pulled his face to hers. "And you, Arlo. I need to be someplace—anyplace—with you."

Before they kissed, he whispered something in her ear, then leaned back to watch her face for a response.

"A door?" she said, laughing. "You put a door on the hut? Which means we can..."

"We can," he said. "And we will."

For the rest of her life, she would. Love him, work with him, be his partner in everything. And cherish a life where she was loved above all else. For she loved him above all else, too. Only this time she knew it, and so did he.

EPILOGUE

"It's a beautiful thing," Arlo said as he handed Mali over to her new parents, Eric and Michi.

She was a child who'd been abandoned at the elephant rescue, and the instant he'd mentioned that to Eric, he and his wife, Michi, had flown in, set to adopt her. They wanted another child and Mali needed a home. It was a perfect match for everybody.

So, after the legalities were attended to, he'd flown to Japan to do the honors, while his dad and his dad's new wife watched the hospital. Arlo was considering this the honeymoon he and Layla hadn't had yet. Of course, now that she was sporting a rather prominent baby bump, the term *honeymoon* took on a whole new meaning. "I'm glad you and Michi have room for Mali in your family."

"Well, if it works out, we'd like a couple more. But having both a son and daughter now makes life better. Which you're about to find out. So, which is it? A boy or a girl?"

Actually, he wasn't going to tell Eric yet that he and Layla were starting their life together with both. Oliver Ward for his dad and grandpa, and Alice Joy for his mother. It was the expanding of a legacy he'd never believed would expand. He still couldn't believe that in another four months he'd be the dad of twins.

"So, where's Layla?" Eric asked, looking over Arlo's shoulder.

"She stopped at a shop down the corridor. Saw some cute baby things in the window and she's all things baby now." Even though her parents weren't. When she'd told them she was expecting, they'd handed her a check and never once congratulated her. It had hurt her. He knew that.

But he had a lifetime of taking care of her ahead of him and somewhere in there he hoped to make up for all the things she'd never had in a family. The things he'd counted on with his parents and the things his children would be able to count on with him. And, yes, in a little village in Thailand. But in a much bigger house, built for them by the villagers. One with doors, running water and real, honest-to-goodness beds.

So, while some might believe it took a village

to raise a child, it had taken a village to get him to open his eyes to what he had. And a village to welcome them both home, with open arms. To a place where Layla was loved and where she knew she was respected. To the place she'd always looked for, the place where she fit.

He looked over his shoulder in time to see Layla struggling down the corridor, her arms full of packages. He rushed to help her, feeling almost overwhelmed that so much had happened to him in such a short time. Eight months ago they hadn't even been together and now she was hefting bags full of baby booties, pacifiers and other necessities. All of them ready to be used in a jungle *home*, not hut, where two baby cribs were currently under construction by a grateful man who'd had his life saved in a tree one day. "Want to sit down?" he asked, unloading her of all the bags.

"What I want is to go spend some time with my nephew, Riku." She pointed to the largest of the bags. "I have a few things for him."

Arlo laughed. "My spoiled little rich girl."

"Not rich, now that my parents have withdrawn my trust fund. But definitely spoiled—by you." She handed him a bag of his own.

"More new shoes?" he said, peeking inside. "I already have ten pairs. Seriously, you can stop now."

"But I found your sandals in the back of the closet, Arlo. Which means instead of tossing them in the trash like I'd hoped you would, you've put them aside just in case."

"Or maybe I have a sentimental attachment to them, seeing how they occupied your thoughts so much of the time. Could be, though, that I'm just keeping them around as a reminder of where we were back then and where we are now." He chuckled. "And for once I don't think you can argue the point."

"Give me time," she said, leaning into him even though his arms were full.

"You've got all the time in the world, Layla. All the time in the world." And she did, because they were both exactly where they needed to be. With each other. Forever.

* * * * *

If you enjoyed this story, check out these other great reads from Dianne Drake

Her Secret Miracle
Second Chance with Her Army Doc
Bachelor Doc, Unexpected Dad
Reunited with Her Army Doc

All available now!